THE KING'S OWN

OWN

Mark H Scanlon

PART ONE

LONDON, PRESENT DAY

Chapter one
The Winter tavern

It was a cold, summers morning in the city of London. Storm clouds gathered like a great hand over the city, smothering out the fading light of the sun. Only a short while ago they had been promised another beautiful day by the man on the television. But to no-ones surprise the weather had changed quickly, bringing about another storm.

The sky began to crackle and rumble with tremendous thunder, startling the birds gathered on the roof tops and in the trees, followed by bright flashes of lightning shattering the sky. While many chose to drive or chance a trip in a bus or train, others were forced to brave the busy London streets on foot, hoping to avoid the coming rain.

A tall, and fair-haired man in a long grey coat and

fedora, walked swiftly alone, his long cane clicking on the pavement. Choosing to avoid the crowds of people hurrying along the street, he crossed between the heavy traffic inching along like a slow river.

He made his way to the street corner where an old Victorian building stood surrounded by the growing metropolis of high-rise buildings, a glowing gas lamp burning beside the door. It was among London's best-kept secrets, hidden from view by old magic. The tavern's front was decorated in black and white, its name stencilled in faded, gold letters above the door, glowing with ethereal light: 'The Winter Tavern'. He pushed open the door and stepped inside.

Inside, the tavern had not changed in a hundred years, with the same decorations, same old tables and chairs. The main room where people came to eat and drink possessed many strange objects and statues, and paintings on the walls.

The gentle glow of the gas lamps flickered in the draft. The smell of tempting food drifted through the air, drawing the many people who now sat at the tables for their breakfast. But this was no ordinary tavern catering to the regular people of the city; instead, it was, a place filled with all manner of magical creatures from far and wide, of all shapes and sizes, able to be themselves without fear of exposure or persecution.

The tavern's owner, Lady Winter, who was a striking woman with long, red hair and pale green skin. She stood behind the large oak bar, watching over her customers.

"Good morning," she greeted the man, her pleasant French accent and warm smile always made her customers feel welcome. But do not let that fool you. She was a powerful being in her own right, and anyone who caused trouble would find themselves out! A few customers sat watching him. He was easily recognized, even with the hat, causing a mixture of fear and admiration, as the legends and stories surrounding him were still told by many to this day.

Unconcerned by the stories, Lady Winter came out from behind the counter as she always did to see him. After all she was nearly as old as he was.

"Good morning, lady Winter," he said, his voice was quiet and rough, "How are you?" he asked as he took off his hat and coat, revealing a weathered face with streaks of grey in his beard and his hair, and a scar on his jaw. Both his hat and coat were gathered up by magic for him, taking them through the air to hang by the door with the others.

"As you can see, we are having a busy morning," she answered with a smirk, walking back to the counter. "Did you hear? my mother is still trying to find me a suitable husband," she added solemnly. He took his seat by the window. He always sat in the same seat when he visited, watching the people from the window. Even after all these years, so little had changed, the same patterns of human behaviour carried on from century to century.

"I would have thought she would relent by now," he replied.

"Not my mother. You know she tried to arrange a marriage for me with a dwarf noble a few days ago," she said coming over to his table with his morning coffee.

"I never liked those long beards they insist on growing," she said with a shudder. "They always seem so barbaric and uncivilized." He understood her sentiment, dwarves were among the most stubborn people in the all the realms, and were never in a hurry to change for anyone.

She placed the mug on the table, the intoxicating smell of her home-made coffee began to lift his mood. The coffee beans were specially grown using dryad magic; nothing else could compare. He picked up the cup. The drinks were all served in the same enchanted teacups, each with pictures of prancing horses running around the base. The pictures reacted to his touch, and the horses began to move. He watched them for a few moments as they chased each other like playing children, then took a sip. The effect was immediate, as the warm, pleasant feeling travelled through his body. At this point, nothing could have ruined his morning.

The rain had started to fall heavily across the city now. The streets quickly cleared of people as they looked for shelter, but the traffic still struggled on. He sat by the window watching the rain fall on the road, the large droplets splashing in the growing puddles. He watched the drops of rain water run down the window and let his thoughts wander.

The front door opened, and a sudden chill crept into the air, not from the cold outside but from something else. The new customer was a middle-aged woman, smartly dressed in a black suit, with short, business like hair. She paused for a moment before noticing him, and to his annoyance, she walked over. Not hiding his feelings, he looked up.

"Is this seat taken?" the woman asked.

"Sure, have a seat," he replied.

"It's an honour to meet you lord Lancelot," she began.

"Enough of the pleasantries I know who and what you are," he cut her off, "what brings one of the assemblies Inquisitors to me?" he asked. Her name was Fiona Whitehall, one of the assembly's high inquisitors, a kind of magic police. She took the seat opposite him. He had never liked the inquisitors, always causing more trouble than they were worth. Winter walked over to the table, her eyes filled with anger causing her skin to change to a red hue.

"What can I get you?" she asked, keeping her voice even-tempered.

"Just a cup of coffee," the inquisitor answered. Winter returned to the counter, leaving them to talk.

"I will get straight to it," she began, pausing for a moment to look round at the other patrons. "Is there somewhere more private we can talk?" she asked, not wanting to be over heard by the many people around them.

Lancelot looked at her for a moment, unconcerned by the other people in the tavern.

"Before we talk further, tell me why you're here,"

Lancelot insisted, carefully gauging her expression. "The assembly has never wanted our help before," he was not in any mood for games, especially if people's lives were at risk. She reached into her pocket and retrieved a small piece of white stone, and placed it on the table. It was so cold, the table froze around it, and a chill bit at the air.

"Where did you find that?" Lancelot asked, almost as a whisper.

"Southern Norway," she answered, "it was originally uncovered by mortals near the city of Oslo," she added.

"Winter, we're closed," he ordered. Without a word Winter locked the door. The moment the lock clicked, all the patrons in the tavern disappeared, leaving the room completely empty, except for Lancelot's table. This caught the inquisitor by surprise. Even she, a high inquisitor had not realized everything in the tavern was a cleverly disguised illusion. The tavern was now completely quiet but for the flickering flames of the gas lamps.

"You were about to say inquisitor?" he prompted.

"Many in the assembly are against asking you for help. They want to prove we do not need you," she answered. This did not surprise him.

"I understand, but not you," he said.

"No, my lord. This is beyond the assembly's abilities to handle alone. Three days ago, we tried, we dispatched inquisitors. We had no idea what is was, only that it was powerful. It was only when our people arrived in Norway that they discovered its link to the frost giants."

"I take it this is the only evidence of frost giants you have?" Lancelot asked, picking up the piece of white stone with his gloved hand. Even through his glove he could feel the biting cold of the stone. The effects of frost magic lingered in the ground for many years if not dealt with. *If it is true, and the assembly has tried to obtain this power for themselves,* he shuddered at the thought.

"Did you hear back from your people?" he asked.

"No," she replied, "their last message was from near city, but we can't be more precise than that. Powerful magic is making it difficult to find them," she said.

"What kind of magic?" he asked.

"A powerful storm that has been gathering in strength for the last several hours," she answered.

"Infused with magic, we can't see through it." This was
not a good sign. He stared at the piece of stone,
memories of past dealings with giants flooded his mind.

The inquisitor finally left, leaving Lancelot and
Winter alone in the empty tavern, his cup of coffee was
now cold. He found himself wondering as he often did,
about being just a knight once again, following and not
leading. At least the assembly seemed happy to leave
the situation in the hands of the order. But Fiona had
requested to go with them, so she could be there when
they recovered the relic and discovered the fate of her
fellow inquisitors. He would have made the same
request in her place. He touched the end of his finger
against the cup, fixing at least one of his problems: the
coffee immediately heated back up. He was going to
finish his drink before leaving. He would also need to
summon a meeting of the senior council, to make them
aware of the situation.

He sat by the window for a few more minutes as
he finished his coffee, letting it steady his thoughts. He
reflexively reached into his pocket to make sure the
locket was still there. It was one of the few reminders of
the past he kept, and a painful reminder it was.

"Is everything okay?" Winter's voice startled him

back to reality.

"Not sure," he answered, never able to lie to her. "I need you to send a message to the council in Avalon. I need an emergency meeting with them," he said.

"Of course," Winter replied. He got up from his chair, and with a wave of his hand, his hat and coat flew off the hook by the door and onto his head and back. He followed Winter into the back room of the tavern.

At first glance, the space appeared to be just a sitting room with armchairs and small tables, till Winter knocked twice on the back wall. A moment later, a door carved itself out of the wall, hidden behind layers of magic. She pushed it open to reveal another, much larger room. Lancelot followed her inside, the door disappeared behind them.

Inside was a grand lobby of white marble and high stone pillars holding the beautifully crafted ceiling a loft, with blacked out windows on either side, with a large staircase at the end to the second floor. This was the true building the tavern was hiding from the rest of the world, one of the many safe houses for the king's order. In the middle of the lobby was a large, stone, archway, cracked and covered with faded runes. It was a magical portal. Winter pressed symbols on a console beside the portal. Slowly, one by one, the runes began to glow on the archway, drawing on the vast stores of magical energy contained within. Then in a flash of light, the whole archway lit up, and began to smoulder with ethereal energy, drifting into the air. An image began to materialize within the archway, a tunnel of swirling colour formed into a picture of a distant land, of clear skies and a castle wall.

"I will see you later, my lady Winter." Lancelot said his goodbye with a kiss to her hand. Old habits die hard. Then, he stepped through...

Chapter two

London to Avalon

Everything disappeared the moment he passed through the archway. The light of the grand lobby was replaced with a wave of light and colour. In only a few moments, he was transported over many miles. A moment later, the colour faded and was replaced with the warm sun and fresh air. He was no longer in London, but was now in the king's country, Avalon.

Lancelot stood in the large, open courtyard of castle, Bragga. Large stone walls and an imposing keep, with many towers at his back. Two of the orders—large and imposing sentries came to life next to him. The machines were among the guardians of Avalon, each made of black onyx and wielding a fierce-looking sword.

"My Lord, please remain still, and prepare to be recognized," the sentry ordered, its glowing red eyes staring him down, its voice not quite human. Due to the strict security measures used to protect the realm, everyone coming and going was scanned. Not even Lancelot, Lord of the king's order and steward of Camelot, could pass through without first being recognized. Without a word, having done this a thousand times before, he simply waited for them to finish.

A ring of stones, with runes of magic carved into them came to life, around his feet, preventing any escape. The magic of the runes checked for any signs of concealment or enchantment, causing a faint tingling sensation across his body as he was scanned. A few moments later, the tingling stopped, and the runes went out.

"You have been recognized, my lord," the sentry said with a bow. "Welcome to Avalon." A moment later, the light in their eyes went out, leaving them silent.

A tall man in a red-and-gold tunic approached Lancelot. It was Sir Christian, an old veteran of the order and commander of castle Bragga.

"Welcome to Bragga, my lord," he said with a slight bow. "The council has been informed and is assembling as per your request," he finished.

"Very good, commander," Lancelot said, greeting

his friend with a firm handshake.

"May I ask what is going on? It's been sometime since we have an emergency session." Christian said.

"Sorry, my friend, but you will have to wait till the meeting," Lancelot answered. He did not want to risk any mention of frost giants outside the council chamber. Now, they needed to make their way to Camelot and wait the council's decision.

Christian led the way inside the keep. Although castle Bragga was not the largest fortification on the island, it was one of the most heavily protected, due to it being one of the only ways in and out of the realm. More of the large sentries stood along either side of the entryway as they passed through, the sound of their heavy footsteps echoing on the stone floor. At the base of the staircase to the next level was one of the Norian portals that linked Avalon together. Magical travel throughout Avalon was heavily regulated for security, but accessible to all who lived there.

With a wave of his hand, the stones came to life in the floor, the glowing magic forming a portal around them, gathering in strength and intensity. Then in a flash of light, they disappeared.

In the blink of an eye, Lancelot now stood in the

courtyard of the king's palace deep within the greatest city on Earth, Camelot. Members of the palace guard stood to attention around him in their fine armour and uniforms. Although not the original place from legends, the new city was home to three quarters of a million people. At the centre of the palace, rising high above them, glowed the tower of Merlin, the source of magic protecting the isles for many centuries. The great doors to the palace opened, and several more members of the palace guard stepped out, followed by the captain of the guard, Lady Isolde. An imposing woman with many years of service in the king's order, she was garbed in the same red and gold tunic and armour of the others.

"Welcome back to Camelot, my lord," she greeted him. "The council is nearly assembled and waiting your arrival."

"Thank you, captain," he replied. The guards remained in formation, up the steps waiting for him to go inside.

While Lancelot waited for the rest of the council to arrive, he decided to pay an old friend a visit. Lancelot left the guards behind and went into an adjacent room to sit undisturbed. He then simply closed his eyes and focused his mind and power on the person he wanted to see. It was as though he was falling into a deep sleep, but his mind left his body far behind as he travelled across land and sea. Astral projection allowed him to travel all the way to Saint Isaac's square in Saint Petersburg, Russia. The square was deep within the city, with busy roads on all sides. Nobody noticed Lancelot appear on the path as they walked passed. The things mortals miss.

Lancelot walked to the centre of the square, where a large circle of grass lay, along with benches for people to sit on. An old man, in a long grey coat, with a bald head and thick moustache, sat alone eating his lunch. Lancelot sat on the bench beside him.

"Why do you always insist on interrupting my lunch?" the man asked with a thick Russian accent.

"You're always here when I need you," Lancelot replied simply. "How are you, Alexei?"

"Getting old, my friend. Things don't work like they used to," he complained. "Of course, you wouldn't know anything about that," he grunted. Lancelot smiled.

"Glad your still in good spirits," Lancelot said. "How are your grandchildren?" he asked.

"You know how it is. Young witches and wizards,

eager to use their magic," he chuckled. "But I love them." Alexei had several grand children from his daughter, Claire, who Lancelot had seen grow up. He had to admit, however, that he was disappointed when she decided to join the assembly.

"What can I do for you this time?" Alexei asked, clearly wishing to finish his lunch in peace.

"I just had a visit from the assembly," Lancelot answered. "They have given me some disturbing news." Alexei's face turned sour, as he knew what Lancelot was referring to.

"I need to know what happened," Lancelot insisted.

"Well, I guess you deserve to know if the assembly expects you to fix their mess. Several days ago, the assembly received news of a relic being uncovered in southern Norway, near the city of Oslo—" he began, but Lancelot cut him off.

"I know this," Lancelot said.

"But what they did not tell you is that we already knew what the relic was before going in." This caught Lancelot by surprise!

"What is it?" he asked. Alexei did not say anything for a moment as he chewed over his words. He must have known how Lancelot would react once he told him.

"We believe the relic to be the Crown of Ymir," he finally answered. Lancelot stared at him in disbelief, unable to comprehend what he'd heard. The Crown of Ymir had been lost for many centuries after the fall of the last king of Jotunheim, during the final battle for Midgard. It was one of those relics they prayed remained lost.

"You cannot be serious," Lancelot said. "Why did you not come to me with this." he asked.

"The assembly was determined to handle the situation themselves," Alexei answered. "There is a growing majority in the assembly who would be very happy if the order ceased to exist. So they wished to prove we could do this alone," he grumbled, clearly not agreeing with their sentiment. Lancelot had to admit this was new. Although they had always had their differences, they had never openly opposed the order's role in the world.

"I'm sorry, my friend. It would seem that things between our two parties are only getting more complicated," Alexei said.

"So, it seems," Lancelot said glumly, "I better get

back," he said, getting up. Alexei stood as well. "Give the family my best, Alexei," Lancelot said, taking his hand.

"I wish you luck. If you need any help, you know where to find me." Alexei smiled, "there are still those of us in the assembly who haven't lost their minds," he added. They both hugged, and Lancelot turned away. A moment later, the square disappeared. He was pulled back to his body waiting back in Camelot.

Lancelot opened his eyes to find himself back in the room. He took a deep breath to steady himself. He never liked to use astral projection, but it was the fastest way to get in contact with someone, no matter where the person was. He noticed a picture of Merlin over the fire place. For all the time he had known him, the old wizard had a piercing gaze, and the picture captured it to an uncomfortable degree. He wished the old man was here now, he always knew what to do, and always had a plan. To this day Lancelot could not understand why he was chosen to carry on Arthur's legacy. Shaking off the feelings of the past, Lancelot got to his feet and left the room.

The great hall was a huge space with many pillars and statues lining the walls. The statues were of the orders most famous heroes and heroines spanning many centuries: William, Tahir, Mavik, Cassandra, and Kole, to name a few. All were heroes who gave their lives in the defence of the world and the order. Lancelot had met and trained them all, and their loss still pained him to this day. His curse meant he would more than likely outlive the current members of the order too, which meant he always kept a certain distance. That is why he enjoyed spending time with the Fae, many of whom were far older than even him.

Chapter three
The sleeping king

Lancelot arrived at the council chambers deep within the palace. Two large, bronze doors barred the way, with two palace guards stood to either side, each coming to attention as he neared. The faint flicker of magic in the metal betrayed the huge amount of power concealed within them. He pushed them opened and stepped inside.

The marble chamber was among the most impressive rooms in the entire city, the stonework painstakingly carved by the great dwarf craftsmen of Nidavellir. The walls were covered with ornate pictures, immortalizing the order's long history in metal and stone. Doorways were spaced in intervals round the chamber, each one with a white marble statue of a founding member, among them King Arthur and the wizard Merlin. The mosaic floor depicted the ancient symbol of Camelot, the king's dragon. While high above, light spilled in through the domed ceiling, warming the chamber inside. But at its centre, where the senior knights of the order and representatives of the humans and Fae of Avalon gathered, stood a large, hollow, round table, an exact replica of the original round table lost all those years ago. Quietly, Lancelot took his seat while they waited for him to begin.

"I would first like to thank you all for coming," He started. "This morning I was approached by a member of the Assemblies inquisition. She informed me of a dire situation that has developed in southern Norway." He paused for a moment. "They believe the crown of Ymir has been found!" He was immediately cut off by sounds of surprise from the council. "But it gets worse. The assembly sent an unsanctioned team to retrieve the crown for themselves, as you can imagine it has gone bad. They are now asking for our assistance," he finished.

"Why are we only hearing about this now?" asked Princess Jossa of the Fae. "This situation is most troubling, but more so is the fact they discovered this before us," she added angrily. When the Fae become angry, green magic burns visibly within them, the power connected to their emotions. She took a moment to calm herself; the other members were unnerved by her outburst. Lancelot shared her feelings, but this was not the time for anger. They needed to take decisive action, if they were going to resolve the situation quickly.

"I agree, which is why a course of action must be decided quickly," said Lord Brennon, the human representative of all non-magic people in Avalon. "If word of this gets out, let alone the fact we missed this, there will be panic."

"Not to mention if the Jotuns discover we have found their crown," Lady Nightshade added. That was the biggest worry: if the giants discover they have found the crown it could mean war.

"Then I think we can agree that maintaining absolute secrecy is our chief concern," said the quiet voice of Sir Henry.

"Agreed. I shall therefore be taking as few people with me as possible to meet with Sir Bjorn in Norway. I would like Lady Rayna, and Morgan to accompany me," he said. They stared at him in stunned disbelief.

"We agree to Lady Rayna, her skills are

legendary, but why would you want Morgan to join you?" asked the princess.

"I know what you're thinking, but Morgan is one of the few people left with knowledge of the Jotuns." He had to admit that he shared their reservations as well. Even though it had been many centuries since the great war that Morgana helped start, people had long memories; especially the immortals who were there, but there was no choice. Lancelot needed her for this.

"We need her," he said simply. They all knew it, but it was not an easy choice for them to accept. She would accompany Lancelot, Fiona, and Rayna to Norway, but he would have to ask her himself.

After the council meeting ended, Lancelot made his way to the large under-croft deep beneath the city. The only way down was an old stone staircase, deathly quiet but for the flickering torches, twitching in the breeze. The stairs were very old, as they were built long before the city. It had been sometime since he had made the journey, and he was not looked forward to seeing Morgan again.

He stepped off the stairs and stood before a large, stonewall, at what appeared to be a dead end. Two guards then stepped out from the stone, hidden by magic. They were members of the elite king's guard, the veteran warriors of Camelot, chosen for their skill at arms and bravery. They stood to attention as he approached.

"My lord," they both said with a bow. He gave them a curt nod, and they opened the hidden door for him. The wall parted, and the light from inside spilled out with the scent of fresh apples and spring water. He stepped over the threshold.

The great under-croft of Camelot was a massive space with a huge vaulted ceiling. Only the most senior knights, king's guard, and the mysterious witches of Avalon could enter. A fast-flowing river ran noisily through on its way to the great lake outside. The water spray filled the air as it nourished the many apple trees growing beneath the artificial light above their heads. It was always the same when he was here, a painful mix of guilt and regret. Even after all these years, the feelings never faded. He had learnt to suppress them, but guilt hung around him like chains. At the centre of the chamber, sleeping upon an alter of white stone, dressed in his royal robes of red and gold, and attended to by the witches of Avalon for over a thousand years, lay Arthur Pendragon, the once and future king.

An icy breeze startled Lancelot back to reality as a powerful presence gathered behind him. He quickly turned to face it, reaching for a hidden blade. Standing before him in a flowing black dress, with long raven hair drifting in the breeze, was the witch Morgan La Fae, as powerful and dangerous as she was beautiful. To say they had history would be an understatement, a long and painful memory bound them together.

"Morgan," he said relaxing his hand. All the anger he had once felt towards her had now mostly faded with time, but the guilt remained.

"It's been a long time," she said, walking round him, her voice creeping into his mind. "and what can we do for you?" she asked, her voice felt like whispers in his ear.

"I've come for your help," he said, forcing back her words and the thoughts they stirred. This caught her by surprise.

"How terrible it must be for you to ask for my help," she said with a smile.

"The Crown of Ymir has been found," he said simply. This caught her attention.

"It's been found?" she asked, stepping back.

"The assembly believes they've found it, and now

need our help." He could feel her annoyance towards the assembly, a feeling that was shared by many in Avalon.

"We're going to need your help if we are to succeed," he said with some difficulty.

"Of course you do," she said, "I'm guessing the council has already approved of your plan."

"They have," he answered.

"I bet. Fine, I will come. It's been a while since I left the island," she said.

"Good," Lancelot said, able now to breathe a little easier. "We're making final preparations. I will wait for you outside the city." She did not respond, as she was deep in thought, and no doubt thinking of ways to make his life more difficult.

Lancelot had already decided that before leaving the chamber he would visit Arthur. The guards standing around the sleeping king stepped aside to let them approach. Morgan dismissed the attending witches, while Lancelot stood over Arthur, staring at his sleeping body. With a heavy heart, he got down on one knee. He hated seeing Arthur like this, never looking a day older than when he was mortally wounded all those years ago, an effect of the magic that preserved him inches from death. They'd gone through so much together, so many battles and adventures now long forgotten by most. He could still remember the day it happened, in all its painful, vivid detail, the day the betrayer, Mordred, struck the mortal blow, but Arthur finished him. While near death, the wizard Merlin and the rest of the knights took Arthur to Avalon, the land of ancient magic and the Fae. That was why Camelot was rebuilt above, to protect the sleeping king. Before Merlin disappeared, he told Lancelot of the future and his new destiny.

"Arthur will return and once again unite the light of this world, but you must hold the line and lead those who remain as steward of a new Camelot." And that was that. All the responsibility in the world dropped on Lancelot.

While the truth about Arthur was kept a closely guarded secret, Lancelot and the king's order have remained loyal, hoping that one day their king would return. He felt a stray tear find its way down his face as his emotions started to twist inside. He looked down at the floor, making the silent vow he always did. "I swear to hold true to the example you gave us, to never falter or lose faith in what you made us. Till my death, I shall serve, in the hope you will one day return, my one and only king." He got up and turned to leave, not looking at Morgan. Then he departed to make ready for the task ahead.

When night fell over Avalon, the city came alive with many glowing torches, and the now-visible energy shining high above, the high spire of Merlin protecting the realm. But this was nothing compared to the forest of the Fae just across the lake. At night, the entire forest came alive with the many strange and swirling lights of their mysterious, magic passing among the trees and hills on the wind. Lancelot stood on the balcony of his bedchamber within the palace, watching the display. He could have spent hours watching the mesmerising magic. But it was soon time for him to leave.

His private residence was very large, with several rooms, but the one thing he had insisted on, was his own personal library. He walked into the large room, in which he kept his most prized possessions, thousands of books and hundreds objects he had spent centuries collecting. Sometimes he would spend hours just remembering, recording history in his own words. It was not very often he was involved in a mission. But today he was here for something far more special. He walked to the large, golden, vault door on the other side of the room, a door he had not opened in some time. He placed his hand on its smooth surface, watched the magic react, testing his authority to be granted access. It tingled for a little, then with a heavy clunk of the locks moving, and the hiss of air. The door opened.

The vault was large inside, much larger than it appeared. Its walls all gold, with runes carved into them. No-one else but Merlin knew of this room, because it protected their greatest treasure, one Lancelot carried with him through the centuries as it's guardian, until the day it was returned to its owner. In the middle of the empty vault, a single, gold pedestal stood. Half buried within the gold, tip first and still glowing with more power than the entirety of Avalon combined. Excalibur.

With reverence he approached Excalibur, he then took a knee and bowed before the sword of the king.

"Excalibur, it's time those who could cause our world harm to be reminded who protects it," he whispered. He could feel the sword react, of course it could not speak but it was alive. Slowly he stood, never taking his gaze of the sword.

"Are you ready, my old friend," he said to the

sword. Almost as though in reply the red jewel in the pommel glowed. With a smile Lancelot took hold of the blade, pulled it free causing a crack of golden energy to strike the vault. The swords incredible power burned through his arm, into his body. Only the power of his own curse allows him to wield Arthur's sword. Only the walls of the vault kept its power hidden.

The palace was quiet, with only the guards around, making it simple for Lancelot to slip out unnoticed by curious eyes. he stepped into the courtyard, the guards paying him no attention as he walked towards its centre, to the Norian gate. He stepped into the middle of the circle and spoke clearly where he was going: "Main gate." The magic sparked to life, everything went bright around him, and the court yard disappeared in a swirl of light. A moment later, the main gate was in front of him.

He went into the forest to meet Morgan. He wanted to be, away from the city so as not to draw attention. He had dressed for the cold weather in a heavy, fur lined coat and boots, Excalibur hidden from view. By all reports, the area they were going to was experiencing an extreme cold front, which was a good sign they were going to the right place. Quietly, he made his way along one of the many small trails through the giant trees. Magic, filled the air around him, causing his skin to gently tingle, as though someone was softly touching his neck. He could feel Excalibur reacted to the contact, as though annoyed by it. People often spoke of the soul of the forest, but he never believed it. The trees started to break away into a small opening where Morgan stood waiting for him. She was not happy.

Morgan was dressed, as always, in black. Her only concession to the extreme cold they were about to face was a long coat, with a fur-lined collar. She walked over to him, all grace and elegance, enough to turn the heads of most.

"Morgan," Lancelot greeted her.

"How long must I wait?" Morgan asked in return, ignoring his greeting. "The Fae have been watching me ever since I arrived." The Fae, like most, did not trust Morgan, especially since many of them were old enough to remember what she did all those years ago. But Lancelot was not interested in her problems with the Fae. He, trusted them far more than her.

"We won't be here much longer. The Fae are picking up our guest," Lancelot said, answering her question. He sat down by a nearby tree, making himself comfortable while they waited. He, was not interested in talking to Morgan, so he closed his eyes and let his thoughts drift.

Suddenly, from high above the trees, a group of Pegasus riders appeared, descending towards the clearing. Each rider was Fae in his golden armour of scales and plate, except for one. Their passenger who sat behind Lady Rayna. The inquisitor, Fiona Whitehall, was dressed for the cold in a heavy coat and fur hat. She did not appear happy either, probably from the journey and the less than warm welcome she had received from the Fae. He didn't care. They all descended to the ground, their hooves kicked up the dirt and moss as they came to a stop. Rayna leapt down with practised grace, while Fiona stumbled off. She straightened her clothes and followed Rayna. Lancelot got to his feet to meet them, while Morgan waited off to one side.

"Glad you could come, Rayna," Lancelot said. Rayna was one of the elite guards of the Fae queen, strong and powerful with her long hair and beautiful features. He held out a hand to shake hers.

"Is that what we're doing, shaking hands after all this time?" she asked, laughing. Instead, she embraced Lancelot. He returned the hug then pulled away.

"Glad you could make it, Inquisitor," he said, shaking her hand.

"I do believe this is the first time I've been to Avalon. Do I get to see Camelot?" she asked.

"Not this time," Lancelot said.

"Pity," she added.

"Come on. We don't have all day," Morgan said, annoyed. The rest of the Fae gathered their steeds, and were more than happy to leave Morgan as far behind as they could, striding back into the air.

"Now, if we can proceed, then I would like to start," Morgan said, not looking at any of them, but instead focused on the spells she must use to form the magical portal that would allow her to connect two points in space, for rapid travel over a great distance. She reached out with both hands and weaved the spell in ribbons of emerald light into the grass. The symbols glowed, burned like fire as she woven the complex magic. The task of transporting them was not difficult for Morgan, but making sure no-one could track them took something extra.

"Stand close to me, I wouldn't want you getting lost forever," she ordered. Lancelot, Fiona, and Rayna gathered around her. The air began to pick up as the magic grew in strength. Ribbons of golden light appeared round each person, spinning in increasingly fast circles, till they were surrounded by an intense, bright light. The magic shattered their bodies, turning them into pure energy. This energy was then shot through a microscopic portal Morgan created. Only a witch or wizard who has mastered the highest dress of magic can achieve this.

Chapter four
In the snow they hide

There are many forms of magical teleportation, each having their own subtle differences, advantages, and disadvantages. There was no describable sensation as they were sent over the many miles to Norway. It was as though time stood still. Everything disappeared in the blink of an eye, and then a moment later, you were simply somewhere else.

When they reappeared, the cold hit Lancelot first before the light, as they had landed in the deep snow. He had fallen on his face; the feeling of teleportation always left him disorientated, especially over long distances. He turned to look at the dark sky, high above. They had arrived in Norway, but something was very wrong. As the assembly had told him, the forest, its trees, and foliage were glistening with a layer of delicate ice, and several feet of snow.

"There shouldn't be any snow here," Rayna said angrily. "They have not been given time to prepare, shed their leaves," she added, sadness touched at her voice.

"The relic must be the source of this," Morgan pointed out.

"How will we find anything in this?" Fiona asked.

"Shouldn't be a problem," Lancelot answered simply, getting to his feet. "Once Bjorn arrives, we'll get started."

A noise from the bushes startled them. Lancelot reached for his Excalibur till he realized who it was, he could feel the swords disappointment. Sir Bjorn emerged from the trees, his thick beard and blond hair making him appear like an old, snow covered Viking.

"Welcome to Norway," he greeted in his thick Norwegian accent. "It's good to see you again." He shook Lancelot's hand.

"How bad is it Bjorn?" Lancelot asked.

"Not good. Powerful magic has been driving the cold for the past few hours now," he answered. "We're doing our best to protect the mortals, but if we don't stop this soon, Oslo will be a frozen wasteland."

"Our priority is to retrieve the relic. Then we can

have more people come and help repair the damage,"
Lancelot said. He reached into his coat pocket and
retrieved a small orb, about the size of an egg. It was a
delta sphere, capable of tracking the magic to its source.
He threw it high into the air. Just as it was about to fall
back, it stopped, suspended in the air, and then began
spinning, pulsing with a blue aura.

"It's found something," Lancelot said. The orb
floated back down to eye level next to Lancelot, as it
waited to lead the way. Lancelot gave it a nod, and it
pulsed back. Slowly and carefully, they began walking
through the forest. It was almost impossible to see
anything as the snow began to fall again, relying on the
orbs guiding light to lead the way, they pushed on.

Through silence of the trees and small gullies.
The animals and birds had already fled the cold, seeking
shelter and safety elsewhere. No-one said a word as
they walked, focused instead on the task at hand, the
black ice waiting for the careless. Rayna was still angry,
and her feelings radiated for everyone to see. Being Fae
gave her a unique connection to the life of the forest,
and she could feel the pain caused by such destructive
magic, slowly consuming everything.

The path of magic lead them deeper into the

forest, the cold air biting at Lancelot's face, till they eventually came to the Alnsjoen reservoir, a large body of water near the city of Oslo that supplied much of the fresh water to the many inhabitants. But not now: the entire lake was frozen solid, along with the bank. What was strange was the pattern in which the ice had formed, as though a large explosion caused everything nearby to freeze instantly.

"I've never seen anything like it," Fiona said, as they approached the bank. Lancelot had to admit that it was an unusual sight.

"I hope no-one was here when it happened," Lancelot said. They followed the bank, where even the trees had been stripped of their leaves and branches.

They were just about to head away from the lake when Lancelot's heart sank. On the edge of the bank, a small camp site had been pitched. Tents, camping equipment, and cars were spread out for a summer party, but as they got closer, they could see the true horror of what had happened. Everything was frozen solid, tents, bags, and chairs, but that was not the worst of it. The people who had been camping were all frozen too, the magic hitting them so quickly they did not have a chance to react.

"Was this caused by the relic?" Rayna asked, looking over the frozen remains.

"Perhaps," Morgan said, examining the site with a curious indifference. "It appears that magic of significant power hit them quickly, consuming everything in the area." Men and women gone in an instant, the power so strong that the residual energy could be felt in the air.

"How could the assembly be so reckless?" asked Rayna angrily looking at Fiona.

"The destructive potential of the relic is far greater than we assumed," Morgan said.

"There are six hundred thousand people living in the city. We can't let this happen to them," Bjorn said. Unlike the rest of them, these were his people. Whether they were magic born or not, he felt responsible for their safety.

Distant voices caught their attention. Coming from the frozen remains of the tents. A faint flicker of hope, of a light in the tent. Lancelot cautiously approached. Perhaps not everyone was caught in the blast. Carefully, he pulled open the tent, the plastic breaking in his fingers, the cold biting through his gloves. He stepped inside, looking around for any signs of life. The flickering light came from a small computer tablet struggling to life in the cold. He was about to turn back when he noticed something moving beneath the sleeping bag. Suddenly, a shape leapt towards him. He snatched the creature out of the air with lightning-quick reflexes and threw it outside before chasing it down. Everyone watched, startled by the what was happening. It took only a moment for them to recover as they drew their weapons. It was good that Lancelot caught the creature first. Bjorn had drawn his axe and was in no mood for talking.

Among the frozen remains of the camp site was a small goblin, with green skin, pointed ears and wearing a thick winter hat and coat. Lancelot pinned the terrified creature to the ground, his boot planted firmly on the goblin's chest. Everyone else surrounded them both, and the creature waited to see what would happen next.

"Who are you, goblin?" Lancelot demanded. Its eyes shone in the light of the delta orb as it looked each member of the group over, trying to find a way to escape. When it came to the obvious conclusion that, there was no way out, it decided to talk.

"Tej," the goblin said, its voice sounding like that

of a small child, but harsher.

"What are you doing here, Tej?" Lancelot demanded. "You know the rules about interacting with mortals."

"No interact, I was hiding," Tej pleaded.

"Liar," Bjorn snarled. If not for Rayna, then he would have surely attacked Tej.

"Why were you hiding? What, did you see?" Lancelot asked.

"Giant born," he said ominously.

"What do you mean 'giant born'?" Fiona asked. Lancelot knew what Tej meant but hoped he was wrong.

"Giant men, size of buildings," Tej answered. "I hide so they won't find me" he added.

"You can't be serious!" Rayna interrupted.

"Jotuns on Midgard," Morgan said curiously, the name made the goblin recoil in fear.

"Did you see them?" Lancelot asked. "How many?" he demanded.

"I don't know, I just hide," Tej pleaded.

"We can be certain they are here for the same reason we are," Morgan pointed out.

"Shouldn't we call for help," Fiona suggested, looking round at them all. But it was too risky bringing more people here to confront the giants, and it would be disastrous for the city and it's in habitants if there was a battle.

"The only thing we can do is find the relic first. They'll be no reason for them to remain if it's not here," Lancelot answered, "Bjorn, have there been any sightings?"

"No, but there's so much snow that, any tracks would have been covered up, even a giant's," he answered.

"OK, Tej. You can go, but stay away from the city," Lancelot said, releasing him.

"Of course," Tej said happy to be leaving. "Never thought I would have to run from giants," he grumbled to himself as he got to his feet. A moment later, he leapt with great speed into the snow and disappeared.

The weather continued to worsen as they followed the glowing orb. Knowing that at any moment they could run into giants had everyone on edge. Lancelot could not shake the feeling they were being followed. He was, not sure whether he was simply seeing shadows, but he was sure they were being followed by something. The wind had picked up in strength, blowing the snow against them, with all the magical energy around them it was as though the relic was trying to slow them down.

They emerged from the forest onto one of the main roads leading into the city. Several cars and vans, with their high beams turned up, made their way slowly along the treacherous, frozen road, which was now almost completely impassable. Even the passing snow ploughs seemed to be fighting a losing battle to keep it clear. The orb stopped by the roadside, spinning in place as it tried to decide where they needed to go next. The unnatural weather was only getting worse with each passing hour. Eventually, even their clothes, which had magical protection for severe cold, would not be enough to keep them warm.

"Fiona," Lancelot yelled over the wind, concerned to see if she was okay. She gave a thumbs up to indicate she was, but she looked extremely cold. Bjorn retrieved another layer for her.

They finally arrived in the city itself. The streets were almost completely empty of people. The cars now parked were slowly being buried beneath the falling snow, even the Norwegians, who are accustomed to the severe cold, preferred to sit this one out in their warm homes and offices. Lancelot could still not shake the feeling they were being followed, like a shadow hanging over them.

"You feel it as well?" Morgan asked, noticing him looking around.

"Yes," he answered.

"They have been following us for some time," she added, "using the magic in the falling snow to hide."

"I think it's about time we introduced ourselves, don't you?" Lancelot said. His words indicated a course of action, and she gave a slight smile in response. But he would have to tell the others without letting their shadow know. He walked passed Morgan to Bjorn, who was looking very seriously at the snow.

"Bjorn," Lancelot said, "we are being followed. We need somewhere clear of people." Bjorn was quiet for a moment while he thought.

"Closest place would be Frogner Park," Bjorn said. "It will be empty," he added.

"What's happening?" Fiona asked Lancelot.

"We're making a little detour," Lancelot answered. Fiona pulled the extra layer more tightly around her as the wind whipped at her face.

"Everyone keep close," Bjorn called out, leading the way. The small orb floating above him to help guide those behind.

They continued farther into the city, the glowing street lights almost completely lost behind the falling snow, but that was not a problem for them. Bjorn knew where to go, and the orb guided the rest. The large park was just like the rest of the city, empty and overflowing with snow. They all stood on the park's edge, waiting.

"This is what we're going to do," Lancelot said, planning out everything in his head. A thousand different scenarios and possibilities running through his mind till he settled on one.

"Bjorn and, Rayna, come with me," he began, "Morgan, Fiona stay here, I need you to shield the park from anyone in the city." They nodded in acknowledgement. As they got into position, Bjorn and Rayna followed Lancelot deeper into the park, wading through the deep snow. They got ready in a large, open area with plenty of space to move. Morgan was working on a spell with Fiona to shield the park, preventing the disruptive cold magic from getting in, and to make sure no-one could see what was about to happen. Bjorn retrieved his two-handed axe, and Rayna retrieved her longbow, and conjured a glistening arrow in the other hand. Lancelot waited, with his hands ready.

The snow blew across the park with increasing strength. They could not see Morgan or Fiona now, but they felt the spell building in strength. A faint light among the trees as Morgan and Fiona started to push against the magic. Metre by metre, the light began to push the snow back, forming a protective shield over them, appearing like a film of glistening energy high above. The snow tried to resist, but together, Morgan and Fiona forced it back, and the light eventually shielded the entire park. But even with their impressive power, the storm could not be stopped forever.

A shadow moved among the trees, huge and illusive. A low rumble made the air quake as a large pair of eyes emerged from the shadows, like a pair of glowing car lights. This was it. Slowly, a head appeared from behind the trees. This was no frost giant, but a fierce mountain giant. He looked them over curiously, his towering height dwarfed the trees.

Suddenly, without warning he leapt at them, his huge, monstrous body shattering the trees as he broke through. With only moments to react, Lancelot threw himself to one side. With practiced grace, Rayna released an arrow as she danced out the way. The glistening arrow struck the giant's eye, followed by an explosion that knocked him over. The giant then landed with tremendous force, narrowly missing them all. The ground shook as snow was thrown in all directions. They did not allow him time to stand. Lancelot reached for Excalibur, drawing it high above his head. Excalibur's blade glowed with incredible power, like a light house to the world, calling for a fight. Everyone seemed to pause, the giant stunned by the power of the sword. Then Rayna let another arrow loose, this time striking the side of the giant's head before he could stand. But the giant braced and continued to his feet.

They stared the giant down. Only Lancelot and Morgan had seen one before, but it had been many centuries since they had dared to be so bold and to come to Midgard. Now they were back and, here for the same reason they were.

"Where is it?" the giant demanded as he wiped the blood from his eye. "What have you filthy mortals done with it?" he added trying not to look at Excalibur, all enemies of Midgard feared the sword.

"You're not welcome here, giant!" Lancelot shouted back. "Return to Jotunheim or you will face Excalibur!" he threatened.

"Don't threaten me, worm!" the giant roared

back, but his confidence was clearly shaken by Excalibur. Lancelot knew the giant would not just suddenly agree to leave, but felt as though he needed to give the giant a chance.

"Final chance, giant. I am Sir Lancelot Du Lac, greatest of the king's order, and I will make you fear my name," he said, his voice filled with the anger, and violence he threatened. His name gave the giant pause, and he eye Lancelot carefully. It was good to know there were still those who knew his name. Everything seemed to stand still. For a moment, he thought the giant might just leave without a fight, but he was never that lucky....

The giant yelled with such force that the loose snow was blown over them. It appeared the giant fancied his chances. He retrieved a huge, two-handed hammer from his back and swung at Lancelot. But Lancelot was ready. The hammer came down with incredible force and speed, threatening to smash him into the ground. His raised Excalibur, lightening hissing along its blade. The hammer landed with a crash, causing Lancelot to shift slightly with the force, but Excalibur would not be moved, and his gaze did not falter from the giant's, as they struggled against each other. An exploding arrow struck the giant, causing him to stumble back in agony, but Bjorn quickly, followed up the shot. His large axe slammed into the giant's hand, causing him to drop the hammer into the snow. Lancelot's ran forward, Excalibur ready to strike. He leapt into the air, and stabbed, burying the blade to the hilt into the giant's belly. Rayna continued to launch arrow after arrow at the giant from safety, giving him no chance to recover. Each arrow looked like a shooting star that spiralled through the air. Desperately, the giant tried to cover his face from the onslaught. With his other hand he tried to swat at Lancelot, as though brushing away an annoying insect. But only helped to open his wound, causing black liquid to run free like thick oil. Lancelot was thrown to the ground in a heap, the blood staining his clothes and stinging his skin. Bjorn threw his axe, which exploded with lightning as it crashed against the giant's chest, causing him to fall to his knees. But the giant's wounds quickly healed; even the great cut across his belly disappeared. Lancelot remembered that the giants were children of Gaia, the earth goddess, and she was healing him.

"We cannot beat him like this!" Morgan yelled, as she approached with Fiona, both struggling to maintain the shield around them all.

"I'm open to suggestions!" Lancelot yelled back.

"We don't have to kill him to win!" Morgan yelled. The giant had gotten back to his feet once again and swung his hammer straight for Bjorn. He was not quick enough to avoid the blow, but his axe and protective clothing took the brunt of the impact. He was thrown high into the trees, smashing branches and twigs as he fell to the ground.

Lancelot renewed his attack, unable to help Bjorn without leaving Rayna vulnerable. He slashed and dodged again and again, causing grievous wounds, Excalibur raging at the giant as Rayna's arrows exploded against the giant's chest and face. One of the arrows burst into flames like napalm splashing across the giant's shoulder and chest, the smell of burnt flesh filled the air. Morgan had stepped out from cover, letting Fiona maintain the spell alone while she crafted a new one, her arms pulling in magic from around her as she concentrated the energy, using the cold energy around her. She did not have long, Fiona could only maintain the shield for a few more seconds. The giant was so focused fighting Lancelot and Rayna that he did not see Morgan. The air tingled with power around her as the snow lifted from the ground as the swirling ball of energy grew between her hands.

"Hold him there!" Morgan commanded. Lancelot did not need to be told twice. The giant looked over to see who was shouting and bellowed at her. Not waiting, Rayna fired a special arrow at the giant. it exploded midflight, sending thousands of flaming shards of shrapnel at the giant, burning and smoking on his skin. Lancelot came up behind him, leapt into the air, and stabbed Excalibur deep into the giant's back, pulling him into position.

"Morgan!" Lancelot yelled as he struggled to hold on. "Hurry up!" He could not hear what Morgan was saying, but her annoyed expression at being yelled at said it all. The giant kept trying to reach for Lancelot while it struggled in agony. Then Morgan cast the spell, and the ground opened up beneath them, to the giant's obvious surprise. Lancelot pulled Excalibur free and tried to jump clear, but the giant was too quick and grabbed him out of the air. They both fell.

The giant had caught the edge of the portal, and the dark abyss below called forth, the hell Morgan had promised their foe. Lancelot stabbed at the giant's hand again and again, trying to break free from his grip. Everything seemed to pause for a moment as he felt himself start to fall into the portal below. Suddenly, something wrapped around his waist and pulled him free. The giant continued to struggle, trying desperately to pull himself to safety, but it was too late. Rayna fired several arrows together, blasting his hand off the edge in a blaze of fire and smoke. He fell screaming into the silence below. The portal slammed shut with a crack, and the protective barrier broke, leaving the park deathly quiet, as the snow began to fall once again.

Chapter five
The crown

Lancelot came to only a moment later, on his back in the snow. He could not remember what happened, only that something had stopped him from falling into the portal with the giant. He turned over and realized Bjorn was layed next to him, his beard covered with snow as he groaned in pain.

"You crazy Viking!" Lancelot was cut off by the sounds of rushing feet and worried voices. Bjorn simply laughed. Lancelot helped him to his feet and tightly hugged him. If not for Bjorn's reckless actions, he would be lost with the giant.

The rest of the company caught up with them. The battle was over, and the giant was gone for good. It wasn't the way Lancelot would have wanted to end it.

"You're injured," Lancelot said, looking Bjorn over.

"I'm fine," Bjorn coughed stubbornly.

"No, you're not," Morgan said, as she examined his head and shoulder. "You have broken bones, and a mild concussion," she said, lacking any bedside manner. "If I don't heal these wounds, then you won't be any more use to us." While Morgan got to work healing his injuries, a simple fix for magic, Lancelot took Fiona to one side.

"Inquisitor, before we proceed any further, I think it might be a good idea for you to wait for us at the order safe house in Oslo and let us handle this," he said. She returned his concern with an un-amused expression, clearly not having none of it. "We cannot guarantee your safety," he added, but he knew she would not budge.

"If you think for one minute I'm just going to leave when we are this close to finding out what happened to my people, as well as the relic, then you have another thing coming," she said coldly. "This is my responsibility." Lancelot looked at her for a moment. There was something about her, something powerful and confident that threatened to come out if he pushed any harder. Morgan finished her work on Bjorn's injuries, her powers leaving him completely healed, and concluded he was fit to continue.

The snow was endless as it continued to fall in heavy waves, making it impossible to see.

"Lancelot!" Rayna yelled over the storm. "We really should call for reinforcements. My people could be here in a few moments to help," she said.

"No!" Lancelot responded, seeing no reason to explain himself. There was still too much risk. They had no idea how many more giants were in the city, so bringing in more people was not an option. He did not want to give the giants an excuse for another fight. They did not care about the city, just the relic.

When they arrived at the city harbour, the once-busy port was now hidden behind the falling snow. Morgan used her power once again to push back the snow, revealing the harbour ahead. The water was frozen solid, the boats stuck in place by the iron grip of the ice.

"I think I've found your people," Morgan said, pointing out to sea. Standing on top of the ice several hundred metres out to sea, where their frozen remains remained. Their protective clothing and spells had not been enough for the incredible power of the relic, which was still held by their leader, glowing gently.   "In god's name," Fiona remarked, as she realized there was not a single survivor.

"The power is incredible," said Rayna in awe. But this was not the time to lose focus. They had to get down there and finish this.

"Morgan and I will take it from here. Everyone else, wait here," Lancelot ordered. No-one was about to argue at this point. With Morgan's power protecting them, Lancelot was confident they could resolve this.

They made their way along the pier, to the farthest point of the harbour. Cold air and snow still blew in from the ice, causing his face to go numb. They leapt off the edge to the frozen sea below, the impact cushioned by magic. Now that they were closer to the relic, he could feel its power pressing against them in waves of freezing energy. Morgan pushed the cold back, shielding them both from the lethal magic. But even with Morgan's great power, it was difficult.

The Mages were all frozen in place, haunting statues with an icy finish. They had tried to flee with the relic in their hands, still glowing with its haunting power.

"Is that what I think it is?" Lancelot asked.

"Yes, it is," she said, gazing at it. "The crown of

Ymir, belonged to the first High King of Jotunheim,"
she answered.

"I've never seen it up close before," Lancelot
remarked as she edged nearer. He knew only too well
that if the giants ever retrieved this, then they could
unite their people, spelling disaster for the Nine
Realms.

"What do you suggest we do now?" Lancelot
asked. This was her domain.

"You don't!" a voice boomed, echoing from all
around them. A monstrous giant stepped out from
behind a large cargo ship. Then three more of his
companions appeared from the very ice itself. Unlike
the previous giant, these were frost giants, blue and
white, covered in ice, beings of elemental power.

"What now?" Morgan asked, betraying none of
the fear she must have felt.

"Hell, if I know," Lancelot answered. "Maybe you
should ask them," he smirked.

"Can we help you?" Lancelot asked the giants,
"Why don't you take it!" he asked, as it was clear they
could not stop them. "You want this?" Seeing no choice
but to do something crazy, he grabbed the crown,
surprising everyone but Morgan, who just watched.

"No!" yelled the giant, who made a move towards him. But it was too late to stop him. Straightaway, Lancelot wished he had not grabbed the crown. Its incredible power burned away his gloves, the pieces falling to the ground, and his hand felt as though it was on fire. The blue cold travelled up his hand, but it stopped before it reached his wrist. The power of the crown could not consume him like the others, as the power with him prevented it. The giants were obviously surprised, expecting him to have been killed. While it had not killed him, the pain was making him wish it had, but he did not loosen his grip.

"Who are you, mortal?" the giant asked.

"I am Lord Lancelot Du Lac, knight of the king's order and steward of Camelot," he answered. "Who are you, giant?" he asked in return.

"I am Koff, chieftain of the ice born," he answered. "I know of you, who once served the great king of Midgard before the fall," he said thoughtfully. "I was not aware you mortals live so long."

"Not by choice," Lancelot said. He could not keep the bitterness out of his voice. "Have you come to claim the crown?" he asked.

"No." Koff answered, surprising Lancelot. "We

are here to make sure our brothers and sisters do not claim the crown for themselves."

"We met one already. Why stop them?" Lancelot asked. "The crown will be used to enslave our people again, giving one tribe power over the others, and I will not allow that to happen again." he answered firmly.

"Then what now?" Lancelot asked, slight bemused by the situation.

"We see no alternative but for the crown to remain here on Midgard," Koff answered rather reluctantly. "This is a secret we must trust with you."

"We got it covered," Lancelot said, handing the crown to Morgan. She used magic to safely hold of it, her hands glowing as the crown floated. A box appeared in the air closing the crown inside, sealing itself with powerful magic.

"We are finished here," Koff said. "We will be watching, mortals," he added. The giants turned away, walking into the falling snow, where they disappeared. Once Morgan closed the box, the magic, along with the snow, disappeared, the power of the relic contained.

Once they were off the ice and back to firm ground, the magic that had frozen the harbour now relented, allowing the seawater to start flowing back into the bay. But the damage to the city would take longer to fix, with many buildings frozen by the storm. Of course, the order would do its best to help speed up the process for the people, but without exposing magic, it would take time.

Due to the unstable power of the crown, even while contained within the box, it was too dangerous to travel back to Camelot using magic. They remained by the harbour for the order to arrive. While they would return, Bjorn would remain to help his people. There was still a great deal of work to do before life could return to normal for the people living in Oslo.

"It's been an honour, my lord," said Bjorn, holding out a hand.

"You're a good knight, Bjorn. It was an honour to fight alongside you," Lancelot said, shaking his hand. Before he returned to the city, Bjorn said his farewells to the others, but not Morgan, wiser men have made that mistake before. They had only to wait a few moments before a large ship appeared high in the sky, emerging from the clouds; it was a flying ship with sails for wings. It was the Temperance, one of the order's ships. Silently, the ship landed in the bay, coming to rest beside them. Powerful magic kept the ship concealed from the mortals in the city. The large hatch opened up. Several of the order's guards in full armour stepped out, followed by Sir Emris, captain of the Temperance.

"Glad you could made it, Emris," Lancelot greeted him, taking his hand.

"Wish we could have been here sooner, my lord," he said. "Is this it?"

"Obviously," Morgan said, taking the box aboard the ship.

"It's been a long day," Lancelot said in her defence. "Are you wanting a lift Rayna?" he asked.

"No, thank you," she said looking at the ship. "I was never a fan of those flying machines. I'll see you all back in Avalon." She disappeared into the nearby trees, and a moment later, she was gone. Lancelot and Fiona boarded the ship where they were given their own cabins to rest in while they travelled home.

Unable to relax, Lancelot walked out to the main desk of the ship to watch the passing night sky, now clear of clouds and snow. The sky was beautiful. The glistening stars high above reminded him of just how small the world was.

"Penny for your thoughts?" Fiona said, walking towards him.

"They're quite beautiful tonight, the stars," he said longingly. "Sometimes I forget how long it has been." he snapped out of his daydream and turned to face Fiona.

"Do you think the assembly will be satisfied with the results?" he asked.

"Yes. Shocked but happy with the outcome," she answered. "I still can't believe what happened."

"I'm sorry we couldn't save your people. It's never an easy thing to deal with," Lancelot said.

"Thank you," she said, coming to stand beside him. "It wasn't for nothing. We retrieved the relic, " she said, more to herself than to Lancelot. He gave her a reassuring smile that he did not feel.

"Could I ask you a question?"

"Sure," he answered. People always had questions for him. It was, the price he paid for being who he was.

"When you held the crown, why didn't it kill you like the others?" she asked.

"It's a long story," he said. He must have told the story a million times to a million people, but he understood her curiosity.

"As you know, I drank from the Holy Grail. Its power is what stopped the crown from killing me," he answered. She stared in awe, a natural response he had come to expect from people when they asked. Most people did not believe in the story of the holy grail.

"What was he like?" she asked. "Arthur."

"He was a great man: strong, loyal and my friend," he stumbled through his answer, not sure why he told her. It was, almost as though he was made to. An awkward silence hung over them as bad memories surfaced in his mind. He subconsciously retrieved the locket from his pocket, and flicked it open to reveal a small picture of a man and woman inside, Queen Guinevere and King Arthur. The locket belonged to her.

"She's beautiful," Fiona said, her words creeping into his ear. He snapped it shut! The picture was not a memento, but a reminder of his greatest failing. Just then, Morgan appeared on the deck without a sound, startling Fiona.

"Could you give us a moment, inquisitor," Morgan said, more as an order than as a suggestion. Fiona did not argue but touched Lancelot's hand before leaving. Morgan stood beside him, not giving anything away about what she was feeling.

"Still carrying her locket, I see," Morgan said, as he put it away. Lancelot didn't answer; he didn't need to!

"Being away from the city has made you sentimental," she said, gazing thoughtfully at the night sky. "Do you still wonder what the world would be like if Arthur was still alive?" she asked.

"Sometimes," he answered, hiding his feelings away with the locket once again.

Chapter six
It all comes down

The ship began to descend through the swirling sea of clouds, stretching out as far as the eye could see. Lancelot still stood on the deck, but alone now, as they began their final approach to Avalon. The clouds drifted past the ship like murky water as they continued their descent. Then they broke through, revealing a vast area of the Atlantic Ocean. Further and further they descended towards the hidden Isle of Avalon, invisible to the naked eye. The great boundary placed there by Merlin himself, shielding them from the outside world.

Slowly, they approached the boundary. The air began to tingle and spark, with the glowing energy that gathered round them in ribbons of light. The ship slowly passed through, giving a little shudder as the magic did its work. A moment later, the tunnel of light gave way to clear skies and the hidden Isles of Avalon.

Stretching out before them were the endless trees of the vast kingdom of the Fae, and nestled at its centre, high above, was the great city of Camelot, surrounded by the great lake. The ship descended towards the city and positioned itself to land by one of the piers, lit with glowing torches. Lancelot made his way below deck to join the others, who waited to depart with their precious cargo. The hatch swung open to reveal the large and imposing Sir Gregory, with several palace guards behind him. "My lord," he said with a bow. "I'm glad to see you all made it back in one piece." Morgan walked past without a word, which was fine with him. She always had a natural ability for making people nervous, and the stories surrounding her terrified most.

"Glad to be back. Have you heard anything from Bjorn yet?" Lancelot asked.

"Not yet, my lord, but additional resources have been dispatched to help with the cleanup," Gregory answered.

"Good," Lancelot said.

"Is this the relic?" he asked.

"Yes. We, better get it under lock and key quickly. We're not entirely sure how long the case is going to contain it," he pointed out. Luckily, the vaults of Camelot had special containment vessels able to contain the power of the crown.

"Yes, of course," said Gregory, taking the case in hand. With the guards following behind him, he took it to the vaults, the most heavily fortified place in all of Avalon.

Lancelot decided to take Fiona with him to meet the council, in order to give her version of events. He hoped this would earn some goodwill between the Assembly of Magic and Avalon. He lead the way to the nearby Norian gate, just on the pier.

"Is this one of those gates?" she asked curiously, stepping into the centre. This technology was used only on Avalon. Due to tension that have existed for sometime between Avalon and the assembly, the technology was never shared.

"Yes, it is," Lancelot replied distractedly. He stood next to her. "Palace courtyard," he said. The magic activated around them, and the sparks began to crackle and burn. In a flash of swirling light, the pier disappeared.

A moment later, they appeared in the palace courtyard with several members of the palace guard waiting for them.

"Wow. I've never experienced anything like that before," Fiona said, looking round.

"My lord," a guard said, approaching them both, "the council is assembled and awaiting your arrival."

"Very good," Lancelot said. The guard retreated with a bow, and they followed him inside.

When they arrived at the doors to the council chamber, Fiona took a moment to prepare herself. She was the first representative given an audience in sometime. Lancelot took a deep breath and led the way inside.

All seemed more visibly relaxed now that the situation had been resolved and the relic contained. The olive branch the frost giants had extended was also a welcomed surprise. Lancelot took his seat at the table, while Fiona stood beside him. Because she was not a member, she was not permitted a seat.

"As you are all aware, the situation in Norway has been resolved and the relic contained," Lancelot started, "although the giants might be content with the arrangement, we cannot let our guard down, which is why I will be sending an envoy to the elves for a meeting." The elves of Alfheim were among Avalon's closes allies, and he valued their council.

"Do you believe the elves will be willing to offer us additional security?" Asked Lady Mori.

"Yes, my lady," he answered.

"We don't require the elves to step in. My knights are more than capable," Lady Nightshade interrupted.

"I would normally agree, my lady, but with the crown now in our possession, it will only be a matter of time before the giants realize this," Lancelot said. He was again interrupted, not by the council this time, but by a strange, eerie laugh coming from beside him, from Fiona.

He gazed up at her, confused. Her eyes were blood shot, shining with malice and evil, as they filled with inky darkness. She smiled at him as she began to walk round the table like a ghostly shadow, pulling at the darkness around her. Her laugh made his skin crawl. The other members watched in confused silence.

"You've become so weak and pathetic," she said. Her voice was different, colder and harsher. "You have let the power of our people become weak. Instead of using power for the greatest cause, you hide like frightened children." Her voice was filled with bitterness. Everyone, including Lancelot, was entranced by the magic in her voice. "For too long, you contain it, and fight against the true power we have." Her words were so strong with magic that they pressed down on their minds, blocking any attempt to resist. Lancelot tried desperately to break free, and his fingers started to move. He was furious. She had played him from the beginning. His rage burned hot. He would not let her get away with it.

"Don't struggle, brave knight. You're going to need your strength for what is to come," she said, releasing a chilling laugh. As she walked into the middle of the room, the guise of magic pulled away from her body, revealing her true self. A dark figure with a blood-red hood and long flowing robes, floating on unnatural winds of magic. She retrieved a small orb from inside her sleeve and placed it on the floor.

"Who are you?" Lancelot struggled to say, regaining his voice.

"I am Hellis," she said slowly, "remember that name," she added walking to the door. The orb on the floor began to spin faster and faster, like a spinning top, sparks crackling on its surface as the energy built within. Then, with a snap, lightening sparked across the room, splashing against the walls and ceiling.

"Enjoy," she laughed, changing shape once again as she passed through the door, taking on the form of Lancelot.

He and the council tried desperately to break free of the magic that restrained them, their eyes wide with fear and determination, but it was too late. Suddenly, the orb shot into the air, and exploded. Lancelot broke free of the magic, throwing out his hands to cast a protective shield over the council. Fire consumed the chamber, flames consuming him as the force threw him against the wall, and he black out.

Lancelot came to only a few moments later, the air thick with black smoke from the explosion. His ears were still ringing from the detonation, but he could hear the distant sound of voices moving around the chamber.

"Over here!" Lancelot yelled. A face appeared over him as the smoke was pulled out of the room and flushed outside with magic.

"My lord," the guard yelled. Lancelot tried to focus on the guard's face.

"I'm okay. Help me up," he said. The guard grabbed Lancelot's arm and helped him to his feet. The explosion had almost completely destroyed the chamber, but his shield had deflected much of the fire.

Although the table was completely destroyed, if not for Lancelot, it would have been much worse.

"My lord, what happened?" the guard asked.

"The inquisitor, she set off a bomb," he answered, coughing hard from the smoke. He looked down at himself. His clothes were in tatters, still smoking from the explosion, but he was completely unharmed. The other council members, however, were not so lucky. They'd suffered both minor and major injuries, and even with their magic, they would need time to heal. Without a word, he pushed past the guard and made for the doorway, now just a smoking hole. If he was quick, then he could still catch Hellis before she escaped.

The palace was on full alert after the explosion, and guards rushed to their posts, locking the entrances. But Hellis was impersonating Lancelot, and she would find a way past the guards if he did not find her first. Down corridor after corridor he ran till, he arrived in the main hall leading into the city itself. Guards had already shut the entrances, and activated magical barriers to prevent any escape. She was not going to escape that way.

"My lord?" a guard asked, confused.

"What is it, guardsman?" asked Lancelot,

impatiently.

"You just came down here a moment ago," he said, looking bewildered.

"That was not me. Which way?!" Lancelot demanded, grabbing the guard, his blood boiling with rage. He would make Hellis pay for what she had done.

"My lord?" the guard thought for a moment. "You, the imposter, said he was checking the barrier." Then it dawned on him, Lancelot knew what Hellis intended to do. She was going to bring down the barrier protecting Avalon to escape. He could not let that happen at any cost. He pushed past the guard to the door, which lead to the highest point of the palace, the tower of Merlin.

Lancelot bounded up the stairs as quickly as possible, fuelled by raging emotions. The faint smell of burning flesh drifted down the steps. He burst through the door at the top of the stairs. Standing at the entrance, he looked down the short corridor between him and Hellis. She was already inside, the guard's dead by the door, their charred remains all that was left. This was his fault, his responsibility, he had to stop her. He slowly approached the open door, experience keeping him from acting foolishly. Black smoke charged with furious, red energy spilled out onto the floor. The residual energy was being discharged from the spell she was forming.

He stepped inside the dark chamber, the only light coming from the sparking energy crackling along the floor. Standing there, before the large, white crystal, she waited. The crystal was still intact, its energy still glowing.

"Step away from the crystal!" he demanded. She did not respond, but instead continued to stare at the crystal, observing the damage she was causing.

"I said, step away!" he demanded once more. She finally took notice of him and turned. As she did his familiar visage fell away and her true form was revealed. She was tall and beautiful, with long, white hair falling down her back and strong, green eyes.

"Hellis," Lancelot said. He tensed, ready for a fight. "Why are you doing this?" he demanded. She smiled, the cold, seductive smile of death.

"You played your part well, Sir Lancelot," she said, mockingly with a bow. "I was not expecting the frost giants to interfere, but no matter."

"What do you mean?" Lancelot asked.

"You haven't figured it out?" She smiled. "We

made it all happen: the crown, the giants, all of it," she said. He could not believe it! "Usually, giants aren't too difficult to coerce into a fight." He knew only too well the temperament of giants. If she had succeeded, then a war with them could have meant disaster for all of Midgard. "But we still have time for our plan to succeed," she concluded.

"Never," he said with eerie calmness, his emotions held steady by firm resolve. Reaching out with his hand, he called out, "Excalibur." The sword responded to his command and appeared in his hand. The sword's edge burned with furious rage, responding to the dangerous magic surrounding them. But Lancelot, among the great's warriors on earth, knew from the moment he stepped inside the chamber that he was in trouble.

"Do you believe you can wield that?" she asked, "you are no Arthur, you can't handle its full power," she smiled. She wasn't wrong, only the curse allowed him to even use a small piece of Excalibur's power. She waited, patiently for him to strike. Suddenly, she threw out a hand, flooding the chamber in liquid darkness that swallowed the remaining light. With only a moment to spare, he brought Excalibur to a guard position, the darkness crashed down on the sword with incredible force. He and Excalibur forced the attack back, the magic deflecting to either side of the sword. But then the darkness vanished as she stopped, and a quiet laughter escaped from her lips.

"I'm impressed. You really are worthy of the stories," she said. But he would need a miracle to stop her now.

He grasped his sword firmly, knowing the best he could hope for was to delay her long enough for help to arrive. With his hand behind his back, he summoned energy that crackled to life. Hellis still had not moved, content to let Lancelot strike. Lancelot did not have long to act. The spell she conjured was consuming the protective barrier that surrounded the crystal, and soon, it would become vulnerable. He made his move, throwing the ball of swirling energy. The air sizzled around it. Hellis did not move, or make any effort to protect herself, but smoke gathered at her feet, swirling into the air before her and forming a thick, protective wall to block the strike. His attack hit harmlessly against the wall, sparking to nothing. It was no use. She was far too powerful for him to contend with. He conjured another and another, throwing several balls of swirling energy while he leapt to one side, ready to strike with his sword. Getting around the smoke he swung for her head, but she quickly turned to face him, her eyes flashed with light, and he was thrown back.

She dropped the smoke back to the floor, seemingly bored by his efforts. Then the barrier protecting the crystal sparked away with a crack of thunder. The crystal was now exposed.

"Too late," she mocked, with a raised hand she snapped of her fingers and the crystal shattered. The energy released erupted into fire, engulfing the chamber. All Lancelot could think as he was thrown through the air was *not again*. He struck the wall with a heavy crash. He had failed. The barrier protecting Avalon was destroyed, and they were vulnerable now. He lay against the stone wall where he had fallen. She was completely unharmed by the explosion and slowly walked towards him. There was nothing he could do not to stop her.

"You failed again, first your king and now your people," she said, smiling coldly. "Eventually, others will see the world is vulnerable, and they will come." Suddenly, an explosion of green energy engulfed Hellis, the power so bright and intense it burned the side of

Lancelot's face and neck. Hellis was thrown clean across the room, landing in a heap against the wall. As she struggled to get back on her feet, Morgan appeared beside him, her face radiating the cold fury he had not seen in centuries. Hands raised and ready to strike again she waited.

"Lancelot, get up!" she ordered. Hellis was back on her feet, her composure gone. She was furious at the attack. The real fight was about to begin.

"How dare you strike me, witch!" Hellis spat furiously. She threw out both hands, launching a cascade of sparking dark energy. Lancelot dived for cover as the air lit up around him with immense power. Morgan deflected the attack with a shield of energy, causing it to blast a hole in the chamber wall. Lancelot gazed out the opening and saw the night sky and the ocean around them. This was a battle far beyond his abilities, and he knew it. The two witches launched another ferocious attack, the energy colliding between them, both trying to overpower the other, a test of magical strength. Hellis conjured tendrils of energy that she threw like whips at Morgan from both sides, but Morgan's protective charms deflected them away. Harder and harder they pressed against each other, both closely matched in power. The intensity of their battled cracked the stone walls and ceiling around them. Lancelot could see Hellis weakening from the fight, and she was too distracted to notice him. Seizing the opportunity, Lancelot grabbed his Excalibur and ran forward, sword raised high as he prepared to sever her head with one swift cut. But Hellis saw him coming for her. She pulled back from Morgan's attack. Taking a glancing blow to the shoulder, she was knocked to her knees. She watched as Lancelot brought his sword down. In that brief instance, time slowed. They gazed into each other's eyes. Just as the sword was about to land, Hellis vanished in a crack of blinding light. His sword struck the ground with a heavy thud, piercing the stone.

    Hellis had managed to escape without the boundary to stop her. Lancelot looked over at Morgan. This was the worst possible outcome. The island was no longer protected, even worse, it was no longer hidden from the mortal world. Hellis was right. It would not be long before others knew they were now vulnerable and would bring their plans against them. Morgan left without a word, clearly deep in though. She was never in a hurry to share what she was thinking. Lancelot followed her out and headed to the council chamber to see the aftermath of the destruction.

The palace had gone quiet now that the immediate danger had passed. Many guards still roamed the corridors, keeping watch for further threats. When Lancelot arrived at the council chamber, the mess had already been cleared, the door repaired and the injured and dead removed.

"My lord," a voice said, from behind him as he gazed inside. "It wasn't your fault, what happened here," said Lady Everis, trying to comfort him.

"How many?" he asked, ignoring her calming tone.

"A least seven confirmed dead here and others in the palace. The rest of the council was lucky, thanks to you," she answered. "They are resting comfortably in the hospital."

"Thank you, Lady Everis," he said, dismissing her. She gave a bow and left. He knew she was right. None of them could have foreseen who Fiona really was. But now he had more pressing concerns. The island was vulnerable, and the order needed to be ready.

PART TWO

CAMELOT, A FEW DAYS LATER

Chapter One
Aftermath

The early morning sun emerged from behind the great trees of Avalon to usher in the new day. Its warm light-belied the feelings of those living on the island. Only a few days had gone by since Camelot had been attacked by the mysterious witch, resulting in the worst act of terrorism in the city's history. But more importantly resulted in the destruction of Avalon's first line of defence, the great boundary. The Order had been recalling many of its members from around the world to bolster the islands defences, and as a show of strength. To that end, with the help of the Fae they have been building a new barrier.

Members of the King's Order assembled the final pieces of the new barrier deep beneath the city, ready to be transported. Helena, one of many young knights now forced to take a more active role. Dressed in her long coat and tall boots like the other knights, her fiery red hair was able to be seen even in the dark, as she supervised two of the city's guards. Carefully they loaded one of the large Aegis crystals. The energy contained within them was incredibly unstable, making it impossible to transport using magic, leaving them with only one option. Carefully the two guards lifted the crystal into the back of a simple carriage with a wooden crane.

Once aboard and tied down with sturdy, leather straps, it was time for Helena to climb inside. She watched the several other carriages around her as they were loaded, each one with a member of the King's Order and an escort of guards. While the guards sat up front, Helena like the other knights was forced to sit in the back with the crystal. With a wave of her hand the crystals surface swirled an inky, blue. Happy that the crystal was stable enough for transport, she got as comfortable as possible. Feeling rather sick at the idea of flying; she had a fear of heights since childhood, and generally tried to avoid flying when possible. But she had a job to do and would persevere.

The large doors creaked and groaned as they

opened, letting in the warm sun. Great shadows moved across the garage as the fresh morning air blew inside. With a wave of her hand the door closed, and the carriage gave a gentle jolt as they began to move. Tightly holding the bench, heart racing, she held her breath. The garage quickly disappeared as they shot into the sky. Faster and faster till Camelot disappeared behind the tree tops.

Helena settled in for the trip to Denna, one of the largest cities in Avalon and an important connection to the outside world. Trying in vain to get more comfortable, she eventually gave in and laid on the bench, staring at the carriage roof.

Unlike many in the order Helena was born and raised in Camelot. Expected to follow in her parent's footsteps as a great scholar or teacher. It came as a considerable shock to her family when she announced her intentions to join the king's order, like her grandfather before her. Never regretting, trading a comfy position in the city's great library, for the cramp carriage she now occupied.

The carriage suddenly bucked, throwing her from side to side and violently shaking. Assuming they must have strayed into an area of turbulent energy; the residual magic left over from the boundary's destruction. Helen watched the crystal, the power contained within reacting violently, swirling and crashing. The sound of scraping metal, and burning wood filled the compartment, as the magic threatened to scatter them for miles.

After a few moments the magic cleared, leaving the carriage smouldering. Her heart racing, she took a deep breath. Forcing her eyes opened she looked at the crystal, but all was calm once again. Annoyed at the guards Helena hammered several times on the front of the carriage, trying to get their attention

"What are you two doing out there?" she yelled furiously, "we could have been killed!" But they just ignored her.

They finally began their descent towards Denna and the cities station, usually filled with hundreds of people travelling to and from Avalon, but now closed off to the public. With a gentle clatter of wheels on stone they came to a halt. So relieved to be back on the ground Helena stumbled from the rear of the carriage, brushing off her coat and straightening her hair. The Pegasus horses were okay, if a little singed, but the carriage was badly damaged and still glowing. Several guards and two of the order's imposing sentries came marching towards them, with their typical military precision. A young ashen haired boy followed in their wake pushing a large trolley.

"Hurry up!" Helena urged as the guards set to work getting the crane into position. Suddenly the sound of hurried footsteps caught her attention. A city official was running over to them; an elderly man with a balding head and tired expression. Everyone had been under tremendous strain since the attack.

"My apologies for not being here to welcome you my lady," he greeted.

"Yes, well," she said not in the mood for the usual niceties. The sooner the crystal was in position, the better.

"Come on," he urged the guards.

"Are all the arrangements in place?" she asked.

"Yes, my lady," he answered. The guards took up positions around the crystal, leading the way out.

The city watch had several more guards stationed around a large, stone obelisk in the city square waiting for them to arrive. Already empty the ring of old buildings surrounded them felt more like a ghost town, the market stalls and shop windows empty of their owners, but still full of their wares. Helena felt uneasy with the eyes of everyone watching her, relying on her to get it right. They stopped at the base of the obelisk, a monument to a past battle. The memories of the dead etched in stone forever. She ran her fingers over the crystal. The warm energy reacted to her touch. It began to rise from the trolley, higher and higher into the air. A form of magical programming, directing it to settle above the obelisk, the fallen heroes helping to defend Avalon once again.

"Congratulations," the official said, happily clapping his hands. Of course, this was the easy part, the network of crystals still needed to be aligned and activated. But that task was for the senior knights and Fae mystics back in Camelot. Her pocket began to vibrate. It was her amulet, trying to get her attention. She placed it on the ground and a ghostly figured appeared bathed in green light. It was Lady Nightshade, her boss.

The figure stood motionless for a moment.

"Have you completed your task Helena?" she asked, her voice full of the authority and experience that came with her position. Being one of the oldest and most powerful witches, she was held in the highest regard.

"Yes, My Lady," Helena answered, unable to hide the feeling that Lady Nightshade was checking up on her.

"Good, I want you back in Camelot," she said catching Helena by surprise.

"May I ask why?" she asked.

"I have a new assignment for you," she answered, "I will expect to see you here straight away." Before Helena could argue, Lady Nightshade disappeared leaving an uncomfortable silence in its wake. Surprised Helena now had to return to Camelot for reassignment. But at least she would not be expected to fly back, she could simply use the portal network like everyone else.

"I must return to Camelot," Helena told the official.

"Of course, my lady, this way," he said, all smiles from their success. He led her into the nearby government building, housing the cities portal.

It was quiet inside, with only a few people milling around. Large pillars held up the chambers giant ceiling, with the portal in its centre, now protected by many sentries. Helena stepped into the centre of the stone outline in the floor and spoke the word, "Camelot, royal palace," and the light was washed away. Travelling by these portals always felt as though you were being thrown through a dark room, but it was quicker than flying.

Sun light flashed in around her as she reappeared. Disorientated by the ride she took a moment to steady herself. Looking up at the clear sky letting the midday sun warm her face.

The palace itself was a maze of connecting corridors, with hundreds of rooms and halls, but Helena was just looking for one. Down a long hall of giant windows and marble statues, many depicting great warriors and scholars. Often, she wondered what the original king's palace had looked like. They had initially wanted to rebuild the city as it was, but lord Lancelot would not let them. Now the new palace was old enough to carry its own memories, and legends.

Coming to a stop before a large, oak door she knocked. The door swung open unaided and Helena stepped inside.

Lady Nightshades crow warmed himself by the flickering flames of the fireplace, cawing in acknowledgement, as he watched her enter. Sat behind her desk was lady Nightshade, a large painting of Lord

Gawain, a founding member of the Order placed behind her. But she was not alone. Sat in a chair opposite her was a young, blonde haired man in a dark jacket and jeans, another member of the King's Order Helena assumed, but she did not recognize him.

"Have a seat Helena," Lady Nightshade offered. Helena took the chair, waiting for an explanation.

"Helena, I would like to introduce lord Alexander Luga, from the order's branch in Germany. You will be working with him for the duration of the assignment," she explained. Helena was confused. She was not a field agent, her skills were more suited for academia or research, not field work.

"I'm not sure I understand," Helena said.

"I'm afraid since the attack everyone is taking on more responsibilities," Lady Nightshade answered.

"What is the assignment?" Alexander interjected, his smooth German accent catching Helena by surprise.

"You are both heading to Iceland to investigate a goblin sighting," she answered. "Mortals have apparently seen goblins on several occasions, which if true is a very serious breach,"

While Helena could see the seriousness of such a situation, she did not understand why lady Nightshade felt it necessary to dispatch two knights to investigate. Apparently, her German counterpart felt the same.

"If I may," Alexander began, "is it necessary for two knights to investigate? Chances are it's just mortals talking," he finished.

"Under normal circumstances I would agree with you, but I believe this to be the perfect opportunity for Helena to gain some field experience," she answered.

"When do we leave?" Alexander asked.

"Straight away," she answered. "We have a delegation from Alfhiem arriving soon, so Avalon will be cut off from the outside world till it's conclusion," she finished.

Helena remembered the meeting with the elf queen, and hoped to be there. But instead she would venture out into the mortal world, a prospect she did not look forward too.

"Okay dismissed, and keep me informed," lady Nightshade said, "and, Helena, get yourself over to the armoury, your mother has had something taken out of storage for you," she finished. With no idea what it could be Helena followed Alexander out.

The sky was still clear with a gentle breeze blowing through the city.

"First assignment?" Alexander asked, "don't worry you will be fine," he tried to reassure her. She did not respond, unable to admit she was feeling nervous about leaving. Having never seen the mortal world beyond her books she had no idea what to expect.

"Better get ready." he prompted.

"Yes of course," she said back, it was time to prove she was ready for this. Together they headed to the knights keep.

The knights keep was one of the largest structures in the city, a vast castle of white stone, and silver steel towering high above them. As they approached Helena could sense the many layers of magic surrounding the building. Passing through the doors felt like a static bath, making her body tingle. Many eyes watched them both as they entered. Everyone was on edge since the attack especially within the keep, the order feeling as though they had failed in its task to protect the city.

Nervously Helena followed Alexander down the stone stairs to the armoury deep beneath the keep, a place with more protection than anywhere in Avalon; where all the weapons, artefacts and equipment for the order's knights was stored. The huge chamber at the bottom of the stairs opened up to an enormous warehouse of many levels. Items collected and stored in this one vault, from the most dangerous weapons to the most sacred objects. At its centre, behind a giant counter was the master of keys who ran the vault. The eccentric Aki Choi. Aki operated the vast chamber with an army of machines, some appearing like the giant sentries and others much smaller flying between the shelves and doorways.

"I never expected to see you down here lady Romanov," Aki said happily, "your mother had me take this out of storage for you," he added searching under the counter for something. One of his machine assistants appeared beside him with the lost create.

"Is this what you're looking for, sir?" the machine asked, its vacant expression showing no sign of emotion. He looked up at it for a moment.

"Confounded machine I told you to leave it here," he said annoyed. But the machine unfazed simple placed the crate down and disappeared. Alexander gave Helena a knowing grin. Aki was a well known eccentric, which many blamed for spending so much time with machines instead of people.

Helena had no idea what could be inside the create. They both watched as Aki cracked open the lid.

A moment later he revealed a dark, folded cloak. It had been her grandfather's, from when he was a knight, something she had not seen in many years.

Aki unfolded it with a flourish, the silk-like fabric so light it almost floated in the air catching the light. He then paused for a moment looking the cloak over.

"No, no this won't do," he said looking up, "do mortals still wear cloaks?" he asked Alexander.

"No not anymore Aki," Alexander answered. Aki gave the cloak a big flourish, causing it to transform into a long, knee-length coat.

"There we go," he said satisfied, "I do prefer cloaks myself," he added looking disappointed at the coat. He handed it over to Helena. It was soft and weightless in her hands. She carefully put it on, over her coat and could feel the powerful protective enchantments woven into the material close around her like a suit of armour, combining with her original coat.

"Impressive," Alexander said looking her over with a careful eye. She felt herself blush at the attention, but luckily Alexander did not notice.

"We better get going," Helena said.

"Yes, right," Alexander agreed.

"Wait, you forgot this," Aki said taking out a

small object from the create she had not noticed before. It was a small dagger with a gold and red hilt. Helena reluctantly took the dagger in hand, it felt warm in her grip, the power contained within reacting to her touch.

"That is Suvi, a powerful blade; a good spell breaker among other things that served your grandfather well," Aki said.

"Thank you," Helena replied. She put Suvi away in her coat and followed Alexander back out into the city.

Chapter Two
Trouble with goblins

The barrier waited to be activated with the last few details still to be addressed at the top of the tower. Helena refused to leave before the job was completed, wanting to see the culmination of her hard work. Along with Alexander they climbed to the top of the inner wall that ringed the palace for a better view.

Together they looked out over the high rising buildings and busy streets. Helena kept glancing back at the tower, but only a few flashes of light sparked from the open window.

"Do you think it's going to work?" Alexander asked.

"Yes," she answered with more confidence than she felt. A protective barrier of this size and power had been tried many times in the past, but only the wizard Merlin had ever succeeded. A crack of thunder shook the ground as the tower began to glow. Brighter and brighter the light pulsed. Soon the light began to form a film of shimmering energy high in the sky, twitching tendrils of light fuelling the shield. Everyone watched as it soon covered the city, continuing to grow out to the farthest points of Avalon.

"Yes!" Alexander erupted with a mixture of relief and joy. Unable to contain himself. He suddenly wrapped Helena in a surprise hug before quickly letting her go. She smiled, the weight of mounting expectation and anxious nerves was replaced with relief. Today was a good day.

Unfortunately, her rush of success quickly vanished. Leaving only the creeping anxiety that she really was going to leave. Together they returned to the courtyard. Due to the leaders from Alfheim arriving soon they would have to take a Pegasus-drawn carriage to Bragga, a trip Helena was not looking forward too after the last one.

Alexander lead the way to a small two seated conveyance; just big enough for them both to be comfortable, and a proper seat instead of a wooden bench. The carriage gave a gentle jolt as they began to move, lifting off into the sky.

Trying not focus on the height Helena avoided looking out the window, having to remind herself to breath.

"Don't like flying?" Alexander asked, noticing her discomfort, "my sister is the same," he said with a relaxed smile.

"I'm fine," she insisted, "where in Germany are you from?" she asked trying to change the subject.

"I am from Berlin," he answered, "have you heard of it?" he added.

"No," she answered, "what's it like? " her curiosity holding her nerves at bay, "I've heard stories and read books about the mortal world," Of course, there were many mortals living in Avalon, but they were part of their society and culture, just without magic.

"The mortal world is very much like Avalon, they rely on machines and technology to make their lives better, in the same way we use magic," he answered, "there are lots of good people, just don't go jinxing anyone and you will be fine," he added with a laugh. She smiled back, the joke helping to ease the tension. Chancing a brief glance out the window, to see the reassuring sign of the new barrier, but now could only see dark clouds gathering high above them.

Slowly they descended towards the vast castle complex of Bragga, its newly built wall now surrounding it on all sides. To Helena's relief they finally landed with a clatter of wooden wheels. Together they exited the carriage into the castle's courtyard, where many guards stood, ever watchful for trouble. But more ominously were the several heavy sentries, standing at least ten feet high.

Waiting for them was the captain of the watch, responsible for security in his fine armour and cloak.

"Welcome to Bragga," he greeted, "the portal is ready when you are," he added.

"Thank you, Captain," Alexander responded shaking his hand, Helena did not. The young captain led the way to the centre of the courtyard where the large stone archway stood. Helena could feel the magical energy humming inside. Of course, she had seen many of these, but had never needed to use one till now. The captain activated the portal causing the centre to fill with swirling light and colour. Burning, ethereal energy issued off the stone. Slowly the swirling light formed into a deep tunnel, leading to a dark room on the other side.

"Good luck," the captain said. Before Helena

could consider a response, Alexander grabbed her hand and pulled her through. Avalon vanished in an instance, the courtyard and castle lost in a wash of colour and light.

It took only a few moments to reappear hundreds of miles away. Now stood in a dark corridor with only the light of a single, flickering flame to see by. Rubbing her eyes Helena struggled to see in the dark, but Alexander had already made for the door. He pushed it open, letting the cool, fresh air pass over them. Helena followed him outside and into a narrow alley.

The alley was dripping with rain water, gathering in large puddles. Alexander led the way towards the distant sound of voices and busy steps.

"Welcome to Sturlunga, the heart of Iceland," Alexander introduced, with a dramatic wave, "two hundred thousand people live within its walls," he added. She took the sight in as they joined the crowds of moving people. The towering buildings were similar to Camelot, but the city felt disorganised and overcrowded as the people moved around the horse drawn carriages. Several Pegasus riders swooped in overhead. Helena had to admit it was an impressive place, but was only a pale imitation of her home.

"Where are we going?" she asked Alexander.

"We have to meet with a city official before we begin our investigation," he answered making his way through the crowd with very little effort. This was no simple task for Helena as she manoeuvred her way round a large group of giant ogres deep in conversation.

They finally emerged from the throng of people to the large central administration building. The entrance was filled with many people coming and going, as they went about their daily business. Alexander led the way inside, following in the wake of the queues of people.

The lobby was huge, both grand and simple, with beautiful architecture and a hard, wood floor. They threaded their way through the crowds to the front desk, were several administrators busily worked. A large ogre, brutish and annoyed looked them over. The ogre looked almost comical in his shirt and tie, having been made to dress like the rest of the staff.

"Can I help you?" he asked, his voice deep and gravely. Helena had never liked ogres, more due to their bad reputation from centuries past and their intimidating appearance, but not all ogres were bad.

"Good morning, we have a meeting with Emma Magnusson," Alexander said.

"Name?" the ogre asked.

"Lord Luga and lady Romanov, of the kings order of Avalon," Alexander answered. The name made the ogre visibly flinch. Without a word the ogre pressed a small jewel on the desk, causing a small, ghostly face to appear.

"The king's order have arrived," the ogre said.

"Okay, I will be there in a moment," the face said before disappearing.

"If you would both wait over there, she will be with you in a moment," the ogre said pointing to the small waiting area.

"Thank you," Alexander said. As they walked away, Helena could not help overhearing the ogre mutter an annoyed insult. They both took their seats and waited for the official to arrive.

They didn't have to wait long, only a minute later she arrived. An older woman with blond hair and sharp, green eyes. Helena could tell from the expression on her face that she was less than pleased to see them.

Alexander stood first to greet her with an outstretched hand, all friendly formality to hide the unease between the order and assembly. "I am lord Luga, " he said shaking her hand, "and this is lady

Romanov,"

"I am Emma Magnusson," she said half-heartedly, "I still believe you're wasting your time coming here, my people have already fully investigated the incident and found no evidence," she said.

"I am sure," Alexander said, "but we have a job to do," he added. Helena could see he was used to charming people, the official unable to stay mad.

"Okay, come with me," Emma said with a sign. She led the way out of the lobby, leaving the hustle and bustle behind.

With Emma leading the way, they passed through several corridors till they finally reached, a white corridor with doors to either side. Emma stopped in front of a door and knocked twice. The door opened and they stepped inside. It was a small room used by the assembly of magic for their officials to travel around Iceland. An archway stood in its centre room, very similar to the ones they use in Avalon, if a lot more crude and worn.

"The goblins were sighted near a local museum," she began to explain.

"Did you interview the mortals there?" Alexander asked.

"Why?" she responded, seeming confused by the question "how could a simple mortal possible help," she added. Neither Alexander or Helena responded to her comment, but Helena could tell Alexander wanted to say something, they would both regret.

"Yes, well the portal is already set up for you," she indicated the archway, "I would appreciate it if you did not cause any trouble while you're here," she added leaving them both alone. Alexander activated the portal with a wave of his hand causing the archway to fill with luminous energy.

"Not very stable is it," Helena pointed out looking it over with a careful eye, "should be okay I guess," she added.

"Sooner, we leave the better," Alexander responded looking back at the door Emma just left. Taking a deep breath, hoping it would not be her last, they stepped through.

After a few moments of disorientation and the feeling of being pulled through a very small hole they arrived. Now both stood in a field of long grass and neatly trimmed hedges. Helena breathed in the cool, sea air and the smell of wild flowers.

"Where are we?" Helena asked.

"The museum, I guess." Alexander answered pointing towards a collection of buildings. They appeared to be replicas of old wooden houses and sheds, part of an open-air museum of Icelandic culture. They followed a narrow path through the buildings. Helena was fascinated by the design, made from earth and rocks with grass growing on them, like nothing she had seen back home.

"Do mortals live in these?" she asked Alexander.

"A long time ago, but not anymore," He answered only half listening. Helena had to admit she was impressed by the attention to detail, which would be especially difficult without magic.

They arrived at the museums visitor's centre which appeared to be closed for the end of season, but as they continued on, a distant voice called out to them.

"Thank god you are here!" the trembling voice shouted. They quickly turned to see a terrified woman running towards them, "I only called a few minutes ago," she added.

"We were nearby," Alexander responded. He reached into his coat and pulled out a leather wallet, which he showed her. Helena could not see what was on it, but the woman seemed to relax.

"I am the museum manager, Elise," she introduced, "we had another break in today, but this time they ransacked the place," she added struggling for words. Helena was not sure what they could do, unless it involved magic, they were forbidden to get involved.

"What kind of damage?" Alexander asked.

"This way," she said leading the way.

They followed Elise to the visitor's centre, noticing straight away that the front doors had been smashed off their hinges. Broken glass and bent metal was scattered on the floor.

"What did you show her earlier?" Helena asked.

"Just a piece of enchanted paper I keep for occasions," he answered, "she thinks were police," which explained why she was so eager for them to help. But at first glance the damage did not appear to have been caused by magic.

"They completely destroyed the front door and smashed everything inside," Elise said. The museum lobby was a mess. At a closer look Helena could feel the magic that saturated the air, and the disgusting smell of what she thought was a broken sewer pipe. "Was anything stolen?" she asked.

"I'm not sure," Elise answered looking around, "I

haven't had chance to check. If I had not gone for lunch," she started to tear up. Helena took her to the sofa to try and comfort her. Quietly she whispered in Elise's ear, words infused with magic, "sleep now," and she fell into a deep sleep.

"Good idea," Alexander said, "now tell me what you think really happened here," he said.

"Well it's obvious that magic has been used here," she began, "and that sickly smell, like a sewer." Then she noticed something on the floor, among the broken glass. It was a crude knife of unusual design. She remembered from her books, a similar design to goblin craft.

"What is it?" Alexander asked.

"I think it's a goblin knife," she answered showing him.

"Now what would goblins be doing here of all places," he said more to himself, "guess the mortals weren't seeing things like the assembly assumed," he added.

"Why would goblins act in the open, like this?" Helena asked.

"I'm not sure," he answered, clearly worried about the implications such a blatant breach of magical law could mean.

While Alexander altered the memories of the museum manager, making sure to leave no trace of what happened, Helena continued to look around. Now that she had the knife, she had a direct link to the people involved here. She retrieved a small jewel from her pocket with a long, silver chain hanging from it, and wrapped it around the knife. Focusing her power, the crystal began to glow. The room grew in her mind, details slowly forming in clarity. All the broken glass, splintered tables and shattered chairs were no longer broken, and the door was closed. Whoever had caused the carnage had not arrived yet. Then the front doors opened and several of the most filthy, scrawny, goblins walked in. Waving hammers and axes clearly meant more as tools than weapons, they began smashing the display cases and tables, taking their time to break everything in their path as they searched for something. Not the most effective way. Then a much larger creature entered, so large was the creature he broke the doors further as he squeezed through, breaking glass and bending metal. She could not tell what the creature was, it was hidden behind a cloak of dark magic. Then the goblins all seemed to stop as one of them raised a faded object, finding whatever it was they had been looking for by the front desk. She tried to see what it was, but the lobby began to fade as her spell finished. The last thing she saw was the goblins disappearing into the back of the museum.

Snapping out of it she opened her eyes to find herself still standing among the broken remains of the museum. Alexander was sat watching her work with great interest, eager to discover what she had found.

"Well?" he asked.

"Goblins were definitely here looking for something, along with a much larger creature," she finally answered taking a seat.

"That's not good," he said glumly, "but at least we can fix this for sleepy beauty over there." he said. Alexander began to fix the damage by weaving a delicate web of magic, like he was conducting an orchestra, as though coercing the broken pieces back together. The broken glass, splintered wood and scattered plaster along with the bent chairs began to move. Together the pieces began reforming into the tables and chairs, piecing together the plains of glass and broken plaster.

Within a few moments the lobby was fixed,

leaving no trace of the damage the goblins had left behind. Helena approached the display case she had seen and read the label.

"What is it?" Alexander asked.

"This is the display case the goblins seemed so interested in," she answered, "the mortals believed it to be a kind of rune stone," but looking at the picture, the runes did not appear human-made.

"Why would goblins risk exposure to get this, surely they knew we would come looking?" Helena asked, but Alexander did not answer, as he was deep in thought. There was clearly more to this than they were seeing.

They followed the trail of damage, and the foul stench left behind by the goblins, an easy trail to follow. Goblins were generally considered lower life, a menace for centuries. But they had not been a real danger in living memory. Scattered and leaderless they usually kept to themselves, away from mortal and magic alike.

A noise from a nearby copy room caught their attention. The door was shut so Alexander gestured for Helena to take one side while he took the other. Helena waited, her body tense with anticipation. With an outstretched hand Alexander summoned magic by the door. The energy grew in intensity causing the air to hum with power. Then it exploded. The door burst into ash as they charged inside catching the culprit completely by surprise...

When the ash cleared and the room was still Helena found Alexander with a small, grey goblin pinned beneath his boot, fighting to be free. Helena had never seen a goblin this close before.

"What are you doing here goblin?" Alexander demanded. "Speak!" the goblin suddenly went quiet. Writhing in some unknown pain as he tried to talk.

"Hold him steady," Helena told him, her keen intellect going to work. Alexander kept the creature still while she looked him over. While in poor health, unclean and baring many scares across his face, there seemed to be something preventing him from speaking. At closer inspection of the goblin's eyes, which were filled with terror but also an unnatural, white sheen. The goblin was blind. She clicked her fingers several times expecting a response, but the goblin did not seem to hear.

"What is it?" Alexander asked.

"Someone has used magic on this goblin. His vocal chords, eyes and his ears are damaged, he can't hear or see us," she answered, her feelings twisted inside by the cruelty, "Why would anyone be so cruel?" she asked him.

"Clearly to stop the goblin talking," he answered grimly, "can you undo the damage?" he asked.

"No, maybe the healers in Camelot," she answered.

"Okay," he said. He quietly whispered a spell and the goblin went limp, falling into a deep sleep. He retrieved a small box from his coat with gilded edges, a mobile prison. He grabbed the goblin and dropped him inside, the goblin shrank down to fit.

"We better keep moving, would you mind?" he asked leaving the room. Helena repaired the damage left with a wave of her hand. The room fixed and the door closed.

Chapter Three
Forgotten in stone

The rest of the museum was deserted as they continued through, clearing away any traces left by the goblins as they moved. But they were surprised to discover the trail did not leave the museum, but instead lead them to the basement. Alexander opened the locks with a simple spell and pushed the door open.

With a flick of a switch several lights to flickered to life. There was no sign of anyone down the stairs, or any trace of the goblins. But Helena could feel a strange and uncomfortable energy in the air.

"You feel it too?" Alexander asked.

"Yes, what is it?" she asked.

"I'm not sure," he answered leading the way down the stairs.

The basement was a large room with many aisles

of both shelves and unopened crates. But there was still no sign of the goblins.

"I don't understand," Alexander said, "the goblins should be here. But Helena was more interested in the source of the magic.

While Alexander began looking up and down the aisles, Helena decided it would be a great opportunity to test a new device, of her own making. She retrieved a pair of odd-looking glasses from her coat. With round frames and unusual runes decorating them, hopefully they would allow her to see the residual magic. As soon as she put them on the room went dark, taking a few moments to come to life.

It was as if a burst of fireworks exploded across the room, crashing from object to object, spilling into every crack and crevice. The room took a few moments to settle, leaving her feeling dizzy and nauseous. Then she saw it, a mesmerizing display of magical energy shifting through the air, like dust in the wind. The room was so heavily saturated it would be impossible for it to be just a single artefact.

"Alexander!" she called out. A moment later he reappeared from the maze of shelves.

"What is it?" he asked, surprised "What are you

wearing?"

"Just a little something..." she was cut off when the glasses began to get hot and sparked. Quickly she pulled them off.

"Are you okay?" Alexander asked steadying her with a firm hand as she struggled to pull them off her face.

"Guess they still need some work," Helena said with a laugh catching his eye. Unable to meet his gaze she nervously brushed her hair to one side to find she was missing an eye brow. Not a problem for a witch. With a simple spell she brushed her finger over the missing brow and it quickly reappeared.

When it came to unravelling magic, there are a few ways to do it. You could simply break the spell using a great deal of power, attempt to unravel the magic, or pierce it. If this really was an illusion placed by the goblins, better to keep it intact in case more mortals arrive. Starting with a piece of chalk Helena began writing runes at the base of the stairs. Each rune sparking to life when drawn. Alexander watched with great interest as she worked.

When the final rune was complete the air around them began to hum with power, waiting for her command. Helena reaching out with both hands causing the runes to react and flicker. Closing her eyes to focus on what she wanted them to do. Suddenly a small crack appeared in the air before them, growing larger as the magic was pierced to what lies on the other side.

Alexander grabbed her hand and pulled her through. Feeling as though they had stepped through a cold shower, Helena finally opened her eyes. The hole closed behind them with a snap and the illusion remained intact. But beyond the magic there was nothing, no shelves, no books, no boxes, the room was empty. All that remained was a layer of thick dust, and on the other side of the room with a large hole dug into the wall.

"Well done," Alexander said, carefully looking at the many foot prints left in the dust. Clearly many goblins had been down here.

"Where do you think it leads?" Helena asked.

"I'm not sure, but I want to find out," he answered excitedly. Helena was not so sure she agreed with him, but there was something about exploring the unknown that was undeniably exciting. Together they made for the tunnel and the adventure beyond.

The tunnel was dark and thick with moisture. Alexander sparked a simple orb of light letting it float ahead of them, leading the way through the shadows like a glowing balloon. Helena carefully looked the tunnel over as they moved, not entirely convinced it was safe, with only simple wooden beams holding the many tons of earth aloft. She touched her coat for reassurance, a strange feeling of dread followed her, a feeling she was not accustomed to.

To Helena's relief the tunnel did not go far, leading them both out into a much larger, and much older tunnel. With huge, load bearing pillars and a solid road of bricks.

"What is this place?" Alexander asked, in awe.

"I'm not sure," Helena answered noticing a statue of a small man, with a long beard by the side of the road, "I think this is a statue of a dwarf," she added looking him over. "Really?" he responded looking for himself.

They began to walk the empty highway with the glowing orb casting shifting shadows into the eerie silence, only serving to heighten the tension for them both as they searched for goblins in the shadows.

The road eventually gave way to a huge cavern,

reaching far below. Both froze in stunned disbelief at what they had found; the several flights of stone stairs descended down to the largest doors Helena had ever seen. Flickering torches still lit twitched in the breeze, bathing the chamber in soft light. But what caught their attention the most, was a giant, gold statue in front of the crashing waterfall, proud and glittering. Helena knew enough about the Midgard dwarves to know who it was, King Roanuk.

"Do you know where we are?" she asked Alexander, her stomach bubbling with butterflies, "this is Alfgard, the lost city of the dwarves, it's said they locked it away forever after they left," she finished.

"How could the goblins possibly have found this?" Alexander asked.

"I don't know, but we have to find out why they're here," Helena answered. The idea of goblins looting such an important place was made her blood boil.

"Come," Alexander said regaining his composure, and together they started the long walk down the many stairs, with no idea what was in store for them.

The giant, metal doors were even bigger than they seemed at the top of the stairs; each one covered in layers of dwarven script, still gently glowing after centuries of neglect. Without a key to get inside, it would be all but impossible to force their way in, which made it all the more incredible that the doors were already open, another question that needed answers. Carefully they slipped between the doors and inside.

Alexander's orb of light hissed out of existence, and the darkness reasserted itself. Pressed in on all sides, leaving only vague outlines of the many buildings to either side of them. With each step they could hear the thick layer of dust crunch beneath their feet like freshly fallen snow.

"I have read about Alfgard, but never would I have dreamed to be here," Helena said.

"It's going to be interesting to find them in such a big place," Alexander pointed out.

"I have an idea," Helena said. In the old books kept in Camelot, she remembered the dwarves used a special system for lighting up their cities. She held out a hand and summoned an orb of glowing light just like Alexander. Then without warning she threw it up, high into the air watching as it disappeared into the darkness. For a few moments nothing seemed to happen. Her heart sank, having expected an almost immediate reaction. Perhaps she had done something wrong, or maybe a different kind of spark was needed. Suddenly a faint flicker of light appeared in the cavernous ceiling, so small it could have been a twinkling star.

"Is that it?" Alexander asked. She had to admit to being disappointed, perhaps after all these centuries it no longer worked. But then another light appeared, then another and another. Soon dozens and dozens of lights flickered to life across the entire ceiling. Racing from one side of the cavern to the other, to make a glistening night sky. Soon the highway and its many buildings were bathed in green and blue light. Now that they could see everything, Helena was met with the most astonishing sight she had ever seen. Hundreds of towering buildings of many different shapes and sizes.

They followed the path of footprints left in the dust while marvelling at the towering buildings around them. It was as though someone had built a high-rise metropolis underground, with many streets and roads leading for miles in all directions. Many of the highest buildings acted as supporting pillars for the cavernous ceiling. Helena tried not to think what the larger foot prints belonged too, at least three or four times the size of the goblin's feet. Suddenly the ground rumbled from some unseen force.

"What is it?" Helena asked.

"I don't know," Alexander answered pressing his finger to his lip to keep quiet.

They followed the sound of breaking stone and glass which echoed out of a large tunnel carved into the wall, the orange glow of torch light leading the way. Carefully they approached, waiting to see what was inside. Beyond the tunnel and star light of the main chamber was a once bustling market place, now turned war zone. The sound of heavy fighting, angry cries and crashing stone echoed heavily around them, clearly the goblins had found something that was not happy with them breaking in. Alexander pulled Helena into cover just in time as an explosion threw debris across the road, pieces of stone thrown like shrapnel. Alexander got her attention to pull her hood up. Helena did so and they disappeared, the cloak of magic hiding them from sight. Suddenly another explosion rocked the ground as a shop was blasted to pieces. Several goblins appeared from the debris, terrified and running for cover.

Helena and Alexander moved for a safer vantage point, aware their magic wouldn't prevent injury. Helena could feel her heart pounding in her chest while

Alexander seemed perfectly calm. He was the first to take a look, then Helena taking a deep breath looked as well. Everything seemed to go quiet, goblins peeked out from cover like them. Then a giant, monstrous troll appeared from inside the broken building, wearing a rough suit of armour and wielding a fierce looking axe. Before Helena could even gasp in surprise Alexander grabbed her arm, leading the way to an empty shop to get a better look. A sudden blast a fire engulfed the broken shop, melting glass and burning wood. Alexander drew his sword, and cut a hole in the wall to the next shop to crawl through, closely followed by Helena.

The next shop was not empty, as a few goblins took cover behind the broken window to watch the spectacle unfold. Helena followed Alexander up to the second floor, and rushed over to the window, eager to see for themselves what was happening outside.

They gazed out to find the giant troll fighting another giant, but the other was made of iron and stone, fire rushing from its mow like a dragon that splashed against the troll's armour.

"That's a golem," Helena said, unable to help herself as the golem breathed more fire at the troll. The troll was badly burnt, but still they charged each other with incredible force. Alexander retrieved a small locket from his pocket, and placed it on the window. The locket floated in the air and began recording. The troll grabbed the golem and launched it through a stone column into a nearby shop, shaking the ground. But the golem quickly reappeared, but was moving more slowly. Clearly damaged from the impact, with cracks on its body and head. Only managing a few more steps the golem eventually came to a stop, as the remaining energy contained within expired.

Slowly the goblins appeared from cover, carefully eyeing the now motionless golem expecting it to come back to life at any moment. A brave goblin approached the golem and hit it with his sword, before diving back to cover. But the golem did not move. They all cheered in triumph, waving their weapons in the air. A moment later the troll fell to his knees, finally succumbing to his injuries.

"Helena, we can take them, and find out what's happening here," Alexander suggested.

"Okay," she felt herself saying before she could stop. Then Alexander threw out a hand blasting apart the window in a flash of light. Together they leapt down to the ensuing chaos below, catching the goblins completely by surprise....

As they fell through the air, with only moments to spare before they landed Helena cast a spell. The air quickly grew thick, surrounding her in a soft, cushion of air, causing confusion among the goblins. Taking a moment to steady herself she scattered the cloud, the air knocking over the goblins around her. Catching a brief glimpse of Alexander as he swiftly kicked down a goblin, while blasting another. Helena turned to see another goblin charging her, face snarling and teeth bared. But she was not afraid as she cast chains around the tiny creature dropping him hard to the floor. Then stopping another from running away with a wave of her hand, catching the creature in the side with a wave of energy, that tossed him through a window. Alexander was a whirl wind of movement, relying on his might, knocking aside one goblin after another. The final goblin attempted to flee through a crawl space, but was caught with a blast of light putting him to sleep.

Once they were sure the goblins were all gathered up and sleeping, they approached the downed troll, his injuries severe. Helena watched Alexander pull down his hood to let the troll see him.

"Human," the troll said with a groan.

"What are you doing here, troll?" Alexander demanded. But the troll simply looked at them. She looked away unable to meet the trolls gaze.

"Answer me troll!" Alexander demanded kicking him, "you know who we are, now tell me what we want to know," he added.

"I won't tell you nothing," the troll said defiantly, "I'm no traitor," he added. But Helena noticed him clutching a piece of rough cloth in his hand. The troll noticed her looking and freaked out, he tried to move. But Alexander hit him hard with a blast of light, and was about to swing his blade when Helena grabbed his hand. His eyes met hers, burning with a fire she had not previously seen in him.

"Don't move troll," Alexander said slowly withdrawing the blade from the troll's neck. "There is something in his hand," she pointed.

"Pry it loose," he said, but Helena looked at him as though he was crazy, "don't worry, if he tries anything it will be the last thing he does," he added to the troll. She raised a nervous hand, the magic flowing out her fingers to unclench the troll's massive hand. The rag floated free to her. It was a detailed map of the city, clearly not the work of a troll or goblin.

"Where did you get this?" she asked.

"What is it?" said Alexander.

"A map of the city," she answered. Carefully she looked over the map, and noticed a name, written over a forge in the city. Her heart sank, a cold shiver ran up her back.

"What's wrong?" Alexander asked, noticing her face turn pale.   "Morag," she finally answered showing him the map. The troll began to laugh, his haunting voice echoing in the silence of the market.

Stunned, neither moved as they stared at the map.

"Are you certain?" he asked Helena.

"What's the matter little knight, are you afraid?" the troll asked. But before he could say more Alexander put him to sleep with magic, there was nothing more the troll could tell them.

"We've got to warn the order. We're going to need help if they have really found him," Helena said, feeling her composure break. This is far beyond anything the order could expect them to handle.

"Agreed," Alexander said, the adventure was over. Helena reached into her pocket, while they could not communicate with Avalon there were others. She rubbed the small jewel on the amulet, but nothing happened. Again, she tried with nothing but the slightest flicker of light from the jewel.

"What's wrong?" Alexander asked.

"It's not working," she answered showing him the amulet, "there must be something blocking the signal," she suggested.   "Then we need to get out of here," he said back. Not needing to be told twice they left the market and headed back to the main highway. Fear gripped her as they ran, no longer concerned with goblins and trolls.

Then, they were stopped in their tracks only meters away from the highway by the sound of marching feet, echoing throughout the chamber. They ran for cover pulling their hoods back up, and disappeared into the shadows.

Hundreds and hundreds of goblins and trolls were marched passed, carrying all manner of weapons like the armies of old. A loud bang echoed from the main doors as they were closed. There was now no way out...

Chapter Four
The stone king

They waited behind cover, as they watched the goblins and trolls pass them by. Helena pulled her coat more tightly, feeling as though they could be spotted at any moment. With the entrance now closed they were trapped inside, with hundreds of goblins and trolls.

After the last few goblins and trolls passed them by, they noticed the last few of the goblins left the column looking for any loot or shiny objects to scavenge from the empty buildings and ruined chambers.

"What are we going to do?" Helena asked.

"I'm not sure, but we can't stay here," Alexander answered, especially since goblins were heading to the market and would soon discover their handy work. Helena checked her pocket for her knife, a reassuring if somewhat dangerous presence. As the last few goblins passed them by, they came out from hiding, the magic of their clothes keeping them hidden.

They followed the marching goblins and trolls, hoping to discover their purpose.

"Do you think it's true, what the troll said?" Helena whispered.

"What?" he said.

"That they have found him...." she said.

"I doubt it, Morag isn't real," he answered.

"I remember reading about him in college, but no-one knows what happened to him," she said more to herself than Alexander who seemed determined not to discuss the possibility that such a thing could be real. In the magical world the name Morag was one that continues to cause fear, so much so almost all mention of him was removed from the majority of texts.

The column marched deeper into the city, a particularly large troll keeping the goblins in line with a heavy stick. But as they followed, the smell that Helena last encounter in the museum grew stronger; the stinking, sweating goblins clearly tired from their long march. Alexander continued to record everything for the order, if they ever found a way out. Helena dared to get closer, wanting to see their tribal markings. But the putrid smell made her eyes water. The goblins were marked with many different tribal symbols. A nearly impossible sight since goblins can never agree on anything.

"I've never seen so many tribes in one place, especially with the trolls in the mix" Alexander pointed out.

"No-one has, not in our life time," Helena responded.

"We need to find out what is bringing so many here," he said. Helena did not say anything, she knew he was right but wished he wasn't.

The goblins and trolls eventually arrived at one of the giant forges. Huge containers still holding the now cooled minerals waiting to be melted and giant vents to stoke the fires. To Helena's relief they left the goblins and trolls, allowing her to breathe once again and moved around the campsite they had erected for a better vantage point.

The camp was a motley collection of rough looking tents and burning fires, many of the goblins sleeping in the cracks and holes in the forge walls and ceiling. While Helena thought the goblins, they followed in smelt bad, it was nothing compared to their foul camp. The smell of their stinking meat cooking in open pots, and foul-smelling ale. At the centre of the camp, where only the largest trolls seemed to be allowed was a huge hole in the floor, but this did not appear to have been made by goblin or troll hands. Alexander led the way up a set of stairs to the second level to see the full extent of the camp.

Able to see all the goblins and trolls now, it was obvious someone was massing an army. Alexander continued to record everything. When there was activity near the hole. A large, heavy crane hoisted up a simple, wooden lift from the chasm. Several goblins struggled to turn the lever for the crane bringing its occupants to the surface. Then the lift appeared with several of the largest trolls they had seen so far, each holding giant spears the size of street lights.

"What is it?" she asked, noticing the expression on Alexander's face.

"I... I think that's the stone king," he finally answered. Straight away warning bells went off in her head, but she could not place the name.

"Who is the stone king?" she asked.

"You don't know?" he asked, surprised, "he is just the most wanted troll in the world," he answered. Then she remembered, as though a switch clicked in her mind.

"Are you sure?" she asked trying to see.

"Yes," he answered, "only the stone king could bring together so many goblins and trolls," he added.

They continued to watch for some time, as the goblins and trolls milled around, but the whole situation was threatening to spiral out of control. The crane reappeared with another troll and a small man, with a thick beard and short hair. The troll tossed him in front of the stone king. All stubborn defiance as he got to his feet scowling. This seemed to amuse the stone king.

"I enjoy your defiance little dwarf," the stone king laughed. One of the stone king's guards kicked the dwarf, sending him tumbling into a group of goblins who yelled in surprise. But the dwarf was back on his feet and head-butted one of the goblins who tried to grab him.

"I thought there were no dwarves left in Midgard," Alexander said.

"There aren't," Helena answered. Suddenly a thick cloud of acrid, smoke churned up through the hole, it swirled around them, scattering terrified goblins and even cowering the trolls, till it splashed down before the stone king. The smoke cleared to reveal a tall, handsome man in a black suit. He approached the dwarf and pressed his hand against the dwarf's brow, his palm glowed with magical energy causing the dwarf to scream in pain. This made the man laugh with glee. He continued until the dwarf could take no more and fell to the ground unconscious.

Helena could not believe what just happened. Dark wizards were extremely rare, and incredibly dangerous.

"Can we go now? I've seen enough," Helena said, she could feel her legs shake beneath her.

"Yes, but we are going to need the dwarf, first if we going to stand a chance of escaping," he answered.

"And how do you expect to do that with the wizard there," she asked.

"I might have an idea, either way without the dwarf we can't escape," he said deep in thought, planning their next move.

The goblins and trolls happily continued to drink and make merry, still unaware they were being watched while they waited for the stone king to give them instructions. The dwarf was on the floor by the stone king and dark wizard, Helena was not convinced their magic would be enough to keep them hidden but she pressed on.

"Okay, I will cause a distraction," Alexander began, "drawing out the majority of the goblins and trolls, and if we're lucky the wizard too," he said, but that sounded more like wishful thinking, but without a better plan she would do her best.

"You will have to get down there and grab the dwarf," he finally finished, obviously impressed with his own plan. "And if I'm right, the dwarf will be able to open the door for us," he added. But this was very risky and full of assumptions. Having already been feeling ill Helena was now feeling much worse, unable to shake the idea of what the dark wizard would do to them if they were caught. Alexander disappeared back down the stairs into the crowds of goblins.

Helena descended the stairs and made her way down into the camp, trying her best to keep out of the sight of the dark wizard. The goblins were still busy laughing and fighting like squabbling children. Many of which did not seem to be happy working alongside each other, after spending so much of recent history fighting. Not even the stone king could stop that and every now and then a troll would wade into a group of goblins breaking them up, or in some case breaking them.

Finding refuge behind a stack of crates she waited, marvelling at just how big the stone king was, covered in solid, grey muscle with unyielding features. The dark wizard was to be busy nearby to notice anything while reading a magical scroll, which oozed power of the darkest kind. He ran his fingers lovingly over the text causing the words to glow with dark fire. He was reciting a spell, clearly delving into forbidden magic that if made public would give him a life sentence, or worse.

Suddenly a goblin burst into the chamber screaming in terror, causing everyone in the forge including Helena to turn in surprise. Overcome the goblin did not seem to realise his clothes were burning. Furious at the interruption the stone king got to his feet along with his two body guards, towering over the pathetic creature.

"Speak, wretch!" the stone king demanded.

"The golems.......waking up," the goblin finally managed to say.

"What?" the stone king demanded, but before the goblin could say more the stone king's foot dropped down on the snivelling creature, Helena quickly turned away unwilling to witness the goblin as he was crushed. Everyone went quiet, waiting to see what would happen next. The stone king grabbed his giant spear and shield.

"Come on lads, who wants a fight!" he bellowed. They all cheered in response brandishing their weapons with excitement, but the dark wizard did not seem impressed with the idea. Helena dared to hope he would join them, but he simply ignored the excited trolls and goblins as they rushed of. Leaving her no choice, but to risk it.

Slowly she crept passed the tents and debris left on the floor, trying to move as quietly as possible. The dwarf remained still. A few goblins remained with the dark wizard, talking in hushed whispers. Slowly she crawled through the filth trying to not think what it was, till she reached the dwarf.

"Don't move, I'm here to help," she whispered in his ear, "can you move?" she said. He gave a low grunt of acknowledgement. Tentatively she placed a hand on his shoulder causing his thick muscles to tense, and quietly recited a spell. A moment later her hand glowed causing the light to bend around the dwarf and he slowly disappeared. Suddenly the dark wizard looked up, clearly sensing the spell, and looked straight at her. He could see.

Time seemed to stand still as they looked at each other, frozen in place. Before either could move the dwarf pulled her up and threw a small ball at the wizard, exploding like a giant firework. The dark wizard disappeared behind a flash of purple fire. Together they ran to the entrance, stumbling over rock and stone. The goblins were caught completely by surprise, but the dark wizard recovered quickly. Helena watched as he brushed the colourful flames off his coat, a minor annoyance to him. His face was furious, angered at the attempt to hurt him. Suddenly he erupted in purple flames, screaming in rage, the flames consuming everything in the forge, they ran but the goblins were not so lucky.

They escaped the chamber with only moments to spare as the dark flames splashed through the door behind them, dripping from the walls and ceiling. Not willing to look back as the dwarf pulled Helena to safety, down a flight of stairs to the darkness below.

At the bottom of the stairs they arrived in a long, dark corridor. They stopped for a moment as the dwarf decided where to go next.

"Thanks for the rescue," he abruptly said shaking her hand, "I'm Baldur by the way," he introduced.

"You're welcome," she replied, "I'm Helena," she added.

"Only the king's order would be crazy enough to come here," he laughed giving her an affectionate pat on the back, "now we better get moving," he pointed down the corridor, leading the way.

"How did you end up here?" Helena asked.

"That bloody wizard grabbed me from my home on Nidavolir some time ago," he began, "wanted me to find and open the city for them," he finished.

"Why would they do that?" she asked, hoping the dwarf was not going to confirm what the troll said earlier.

"They want to free Morag and take the city for themselves," he answered glumly. Helena went quiet, unable to speak. Baldur looked at her. "You know?" he asked surprised.

"We interrogated a troll, I just hoped it was a lie" she answered.

"Afraid not, Morag is very real," Baldur said, "but lucky for us the door is still closed," he said. They went into a large room, with gilded walls and ceiling, and ornate decorations surrounding a large, golden throne set a top a marble base. It was among the most beautiful things Helena had ever seen, a monument to a past king of Alfgard.

Baldur went to the throne while Helena waited by the door, checking the corridor for any sign of the goblins. He disappeared behind the throne as he looked for something. She was about to say something when he reappeared with a large key.

"Found it," he said brandishing it, "we need to get back to the entrance," he added leading the way out.

"Good, my friend should be waiting for us there," she said chasing after him.

There was no sign of pursuit, no sound of coming feet or rattling armour. Slowly they emerged back out into the highway, where it was deathly quiet. The illuminated ceiling Helena had ignited earlier was now dark. Now only the faint glow of torches flickered in the shadows, left behind by the goblins who came through earlier. Keeping out of sight they moved quickly towards the entrance, Helena relying on Baldur to lead the way.

"Where is your friend?" Baldur asked as they took cover near the entrance, trying to see Alexander. But he was nowhere to be seen.

"I don't know, he is supposed to be here," she answered.

"We can't wait around," Baldur insisted. But Helena was not about to abandon him now. Her thoughts were interrupted by the appearance of the stone king and his guards. Soon goblins also started to pour in from all directions, surrounding the highway from all sides. Then the dark wizard appeared leading Alexander to the centre of the throng and threw him to the floor.

Shocked, she watched the goblins and trolls jeer and laugh at Alexander, some even throwing food at him. Everything had gone wrong; how could they escape now.

"I know you're here!" the stone king yelled into the darkness, "hand yourself over or the human dies!" he threatened. The wizard threw a lash of lightening and struck Alexander's back causing him to scream in pain, his clothes burned with smoke. If not for Baldur holding her arms, she would have given up then and there.

"No, if you go out there, they will kill you both," he snapped at her.

"I can't just leave him," she insisted, a mixture of anger and desperation clouding her judgment.

"We need to be smart," Baldur said watching the goblins, who now numbered in the thousands around them.

"What then?" she asked.

"I will buy you time, you must open the door," Baldur said giving her the key.

"But they have it surrounded, I will never get close with the dark wizard there," she said.

"The key is not for that door, now go," he said pointing at a large, stone archway built into the cavern wall. Now that she looked at it, it was obviously a kind of portal. Baldur stepped out and brushed away the invisible magic she placed on him, letting the stone king see him.

Surrounded by giants Baldur walked straight towards the stone king.

"Hey baldy!" Baldur yelled at the stone king. Helena seized the opportunity and ran across the road, avoiding the gaze of everyone there. The goblins and trolls had gone quiet as they waited for the stone king to speak. Helena reached the archway, at least two dozen feet high and nearly half across. But she could not see a place for a key, she glanced back at Baldur in time to see the goblins pounce on him, pinning him to the floor as though scared he would escape again. Frantically she looked for a key hole, but the archway was so large it could take hours to find it. Suddenly the key began to glow in her hand, causing the archway to glow in return. With a crackle of energy everyone turned to see as the archway filled with light, stinging the air.

"Run girl, get out of there!" Baldur screamed from beneath the goblins. Helena ran for cover just as the archway exploded with energy, stripping away her invisibility magic. The wash of blue, swirling energy flushed out then sucked back in. Taking cover behind a column Helena watched.

Everyone waited, silent and confused. But then people began marching out from the portal, first a dozen, then two dozen. All dwarves like Baldur, but in heavy armour, glowing with protective magic, and carrying deadly weapons. Baldur never meant for them to escape, he was bringing help to them. Over a hundred of Nidavlir's finest warriors took up formation in front of the stone king. Then a final dwarf marched out, flanked by his personal guard. Clad in gold and silver, wielding a large hammer.

Chapter Five
The battle for Alfgard

The arrival of the dwarves had changed everything. Both sides now stood facing one another, waiting to see who would make the first move. While the stone king had been caught by surprise, he soon rallied his forces. The goblins and trolls gathered into an angry mass facing the dwarves, more terrified of their leader than their foe. They snarled angrily at the dwarves, thrusting their weapons threateningly and beating their chests. But the dwarves, happy to let them get ready, stood motionless, without a sound, faces hidden behind golden masks. Their leader walked out in front.

"I am Lord Rhudan!" he yelled, his voice strong and forceful, "release my nephew and leave this place!" he commanded. The stone king pushed his way to the front of his mob, closely followed by the dark wizard.

"You dare command me? I am the stone king and this is my domain!" he shot back. But Rhudan was unimpressed.

Seizing the opportunity, Helena made her way to Alexander and Baldur who were only guarded by a few goblins and a large troll at the rear of the mob. No-one noticed her move behind them. Only feet away from her companions, she needed to lure the troll away before freeing them. With a wave of her hand a small, glowing pixie sparked to life. The little pixie flew round the troll's head, like an annoying insect stinging his face. The troll took a swing, but missed. With each attempt he made to swat it, the angrier he got. The simple-minded troll followed the pixie away from her friends and soon disappeared down a corridor, followed by a heavy fall as he missed the dark steps. Helena cringed, unable to stop herself feeling sorry for the creature.

Quickly she rushed over to Alexander and Baldur. Both were bound by the dark wizard's magic.

"Are you okay?" she asked Alexander.

"Peachy..." he answered half-heartedly, but Baldur hushed him. The last thing they needed was to draw the goblins attention. The ropes around their wrists were conjured from dark magic, stopping

Alexander from using magic to free himself. Helena would need to find a way to unravel the magic. But then she remembered her knife still hidden away in her coat. She pulled it free, the gold blade glinting in the light. The blade easily cut through the rope causing sparks to spit off, burning her hand. Once Alexander was free, she quickly cut the ropes on Baldur when a terrible scream made the hairs on her neck stand on end. They all froze.

A goblin had seen her freeing them and tried to get the attention of his fellows, but had only caused confusion among the mob. They thought the dwarves were attacking. Baldur rushed forward and hammered the goblin to the ground with his mighty fists, but the damage was done and all sense of restraint gone. The goblins and trolls all charged forward; undisciplined and uncoordinated they stampeded, not even the stone king could stop them now.

The dwarves stood their ground and assembled their formation along the highway with the military precision of a professional army. A wall of shields, with axes and spears waited for the oncoming charge. But Helena could not see how they hoped to survive the wave of muscle and sinew coming their way. Suddenly small bolts of silver steel whistled from behind the dwarf's front ranks, dropping dozens of goblins, breaking the charge as they stumbled over the dead and wounded. Then they crashed, the deafening sound of bashing metal and splintered wood echoed around them. Baldur grabbed Helena who stood frozen in place, watching the battle unfold. But their escape had not gone unnoticed by the stone king, who watched them run.

Desperate to keep his prisoners he ordered a handful of goblins and a troll after them, while he watched the battle unfold.

"Come on," Baldur urged, while helping Alexander move. Helena only noticed now just how pale Alexander was, his eyes blood shot and hands shaking. The goblins were closing in on them, coming from all sides to try and cut them off. Suddenly a spear was thrown, narrowly missing them.

"You have nowhere to go witch," a goblin sneered. She could feel his dark thoughts, the violence and pain he promised her. "We only want the dwarf. We'll let you go if you hand him over," he said. A goblin launched himself from the shadows at her. With no time to think, adrenaline sharpening her mind, she threw out a hand and the goblin disappeared in a cloud of ash. They all stared at the cloud of ash as it cleared. The goblin was gone.

The goblins paused their attack, looking at each other, their enthusiasm replaced with fear. But the troll slammed his hammer against the floor in anger, and shoved the others forward. Helena raised both hands, casting a web of magic, and snaring the goblins together in ropes of light, but the troll kept coming, breaking through the magic. Raising his weapon high the troll swung for her. In a last-ditch effort Helena cast a shield over them, the umbrella of energy protecting them. The troll struck the shield as hard as he could, with no success. Angered the troll hit the shield again and again, snarling as he grew more and more angry with each attempt, but the shield held. The wall behind them suddenly exploded. Rocks and shrapnel thrown all around them, and the shield disappeared as she lost focus.

As the dust settled a huge figure loomed over them. She tried to clear her eye, but could only see the blurred figure, much larger than any troll. Its huge, stony hand picked her up, placing her on its back with Alexander. Still struggling to see she rubbed her eyes. Then she saw it. They were astride a giant golem with

Baldur as he directed it. Baldur faced down the mighty troll with a glowing sword in the golem's hand. Their weapons clashed again and again with tremendous force. The trolls hammer starting to break under the onslaught. Helena turned to Alexander who was not looking good, with one hand she held onto him while the other kept her steady.

Baldur continued to fight the troll, who was clearly no ordinary, dim-witted beast, like the rest. He was hiding a keen intelligence behind his animal snarls and bellows of rage, but Baldur was getting the better of him; the troll did not have the stamina of the golem. Throwing caution to the wind the troll leapt onto the golem trying to get at Baldur, but the move only served to impale him on the golem's blade, burying itself to the hilt. The troll stared at them all in surprise as it slowly fell to the floor.

"Are you two okay back there?" Baldur yelled.

"Yes," Helena responded.

"I will find help," Baldur said, and he began marching the golem.

Baldur did his best to skirt the battle. The echoing screams of fighting dwarves and goblins, beating metal and screams of pain filled the air. It felt as though she was trapped in a nightmare, watching as the fight grew more and more frantic. Dwarves pressed the goblins and trolls harder, with an ever-growing mound of fallen warriors; the memory of which would haunt Helena for the rest of her life. Suddenly a crack of thunder and a flash of lighting filled the highway. They turned to see the dark wizard throwing aside a group of dwarves who got too close.

"Not so fast," the dark wizard said seeing them.

"I hoped you would still be here," Baldur said threateningly, "once my brothers are finished with the stone king, they will want words with you," he added.

"Don't threaten me dwarf, your people are nothing compared to me." he snapped. He turned to his attention to Helena, "kings order I suppose," he said. "Now if you don't mind handing the dwarf over, he has a little door to open for me," he added.

"No," Helena said defiantly, "you can't have him," she added.

Baldur charged the golem forward, but before they knew what happened the dark wizard disappeared into the shadows. Then a moment later reappeared on the golem with them, and with a wave of his hand threw them all to the ground. Helena landed roughly, her coat protecting her from the hard stone. Quickly she got to her feet just in time to see Baldur grab one of the goblins weapons and throw it at the dark wizard, but the spear simply passed through him, as though he was a ghost. With a wave of his hand Baldur was thrown into the darkness. Helena now stood alone.

She could not see Baldur or Alexander. The dark wizard seemed to be sizing her up, gauging her power, unsure what to do with her.

"Who are you?" she asked, trying to buy time, hoping for a miracle.

"My name is Felix," he answered with a mocking bow, "now please surrender and I will make your death painless," he said, as though Helena would accept the offer.

"Very well," he said, a smile creeping into his face. He slowly reached out both hands. Fire sparked to life between his palms, gathering in swirling flames.

Her mind worked quickly to think of a counter to his choice of magic. Water was the obvious choice but there was so little. She did her best to gather moisture from the air, moving her hands in a hypnotic motion as they formed into droplets of water, swirling with tides of energy. Felix watched with great interest, keen to see what she would do next.

Then he threw the fire at her. Reacting quickly, she stretched the water out in front of her forming a protective wall. The fire splashed against the water and exploded filling the air with steam. Stunned by the explosion, she covered her eyes. But the moment she did Felix grabbed at her with an invisible web of magic and threw her against a stone pillar. Dazed and on her back, she stared up at the dark ceiling.

"Not bad little witch," Felix laughed.

She struggled back to her feet, covered in water but burning with anger. Calling on more power than ever before. All restraint gone she threw out both hands, latching onto the nearby building with telekinetic power and pulled. Felix did not move, but simply watched her work.

The buildings broke, and tumbling stones and falling timber crashed down on him. But as the debris fell on him his defensive charms simply flashed to life leaving him merely covered in a fine dust.

"You have potential, but you will have to do better than that," he mocked brushing the dust off. He stepped back into the shadows and disappeared. The last thing she saw was his eyes as they flashed away. Confused for a moment Helena looked for him, but there was no way to see through his shadowy magic. Dealing with invisibility was never easy, but she had read plenty of books, and had been trained. All sound from the battle and flickering light disappeared. She conjured an orb of bright light, the energy sensing her emotions as she began to feed it more and more power.

"What are you doing, you can't beat the dark," Felix mocked, his voice trying to creep into her mind. Able to sense his movement around her as he circled, toying with her. Then she heard it. A spark of fire, a flicker of flame. Closing her eyes tightly she threw the orb high into the air, and it exploded. The darkness was driven back by the blinding light, so bright as to nearly blind her through closed eyes. She stepped back just in time to avoid the spout of badly aimed fire, burning the air in front of her. Felix groaned in blind agony as he stumbled around. Helena spun on the spot, throwing out both hands. She could not see but heard the blast of wind throw Felix into the shadows with a muffled thump.

"Clever," he said dropping the vale of magic hiding him, "it's a shame you're on the wrong side," he added.

"Who do you work for?" Helena asked.

"You will find out soon enough," he answered.

They both stood watching each other, but it was obvious to Helena that there was no way she could beat Felix. He was playing with her.

"I have to admit, I have enjoyed our game," he said with a dangerous smile, "but time to bring this to an end," he added. Defiance now her default she stood her ground and drew her knife.

"You can't be serious," he said surprised.

"Trust me, she is," the voice surprised them both. Felix turned to find Alexander behind him. Before Felix could react, Alexander struck him with a large piece of magically infused timber which exploded through his protective charms. Felix was thrown to the ground.

"Surrender!" Alexander demanded. But even with blood running from his nose and mouth Felix grinned at them. Suddenly he wrapped himself in darkness and disappeared.

"Where did he go?" Alexander asked looking round.

"I think I know," Helena replied, "He must be going for the door beneath the forge."

"Get after him!" Alexander said staggering to a

pillar. Helena hesitated, how was she supposed to stop him, he clearly demonstrated his power. Alexander noticed.

"Helena, you're a knight and you're all that stands in his way," he said, "go, it's your turn to be the hero," he added. Helena took a deep breath, part of her not wanting to leave him, but she forced herself to turn away and ran for the forge, brushing aside a single tear.

The battle between the dwarves and the stone king's mob was coming to its conclusion to Helena's relief. The dwarves were winning, forcing the remaining trolls and goblins up against the entrance, leaving piles of the dead behind them. Helena watched it play out until she entered the forge, unable to believe the stone king kept fighting.

Inside the forge was quiet. All but one of the many goblins and trolls were gone, staggering around the deserted camp, drinking the booze instead of fighting. There was no sign of Felix but for the flickering torches glowing from the hole. She crept to the edge of the hole, deciding to leave the drunk goblin, who was now singing and peered over. A wooden stair case lead to the bottom with the lift. Taking a deep breath, she stepped off the edge and disappeared into the shadows down below.

Chapter Six
Morag

Helena landed at the base of the hole. A heavy layer of dust blasted up around her as she stopped her fall, with a cushion of air. She gazed into the gloom ahead, a large tunnel had been dug out with rough looking timbers holding up the ceiling. But at the end of the tunnel, covered in mud and grime was a large door, almost as big as the entrance to Alfgard still partially buried. Felix was stood before it, gazing longingly at the runes, but luckily still unable to find a way inside.

Slowly Helena approached the dark wizard. He seemed oblivious to her as he carefully looked the runes over. The door was a wonder of design, like nothing Helena had ever seen, and even more impressive than the city above. Made of the black adamant and covered in strange symbols Helena did not recognise. The door was clearly not made by the dwarves.

"What do you think? Made by the Vanir, you know" Felix suddenly said turning to face her, "marvellous, isn't it," he added.

"I won't let you open it," she said firmly.

"Really?" he said in mock surprise, "don't you get tired of it all, the secrecy and isolation of our world," he said, his words trying to worm their way into her mind. "We fight the battles mortals can't to keep them safe, and what do we get," a deep-seated pain revealing in his voice, "It doesn't have to be that way, we can have a new world, a world of magic," he added. She had read the stories of what it cost the last time people like him tried. All that fighting was the cost, Alexander, Baldur, they were the cost.

"No," she said with a calmness that caught Felix off guard.

Neither moved, both anchored in place as they stared each other down. Felix was surprised by Helena's fire, unable to bully her into submission.

Suddenly the quiet was rocked by an explosion from above. The ceiling cracked and shifted causing loose earth to fall around them. But still they did not move, Helena fighting her instincts to run for cover, but knowing if she did Felix would strike. Another loud crash of thunder rocked the tunnel, but this time it came from the other side of the door. Morag could sense their presence. Suddenly Felix turned and ran for the door. Helena blasted the ceiling above him with a flash of light. Tons of earth and stone came crashing down on him, filling the air with dust until nothing could be seen. Where Felix had been only moments ago was completely buried. Surely not even he could have survived that. But then she heard it, the creaking of metal.

Stunned Helena watched as the fallen earth and rocks started to move towards her, followed by intense heat so hot the earth was burned and cracked. Slowly she backed away, throwing a shield in front of her, the umbrella of energy glistened as the heat pressed against it. Then the earth exploded, blasting debris. The shield protected her, the swirling dust and shattered rocks thrown around her.

Buried under earth by the explosion, she struggling to her feet pushing aside the dirt. Somehow Felix had succeeded, the door was open.

In the door way, larger than any troll and more terrifying than anything she could imagine, was Morag. A giant man covered in flickering flames. With each heavy step the ground burned and cracked.

"Finally, I am free," he said. His voice boomed deeply over her, his breath licked the air with twitching flames.

Helena had seen enough, time to run. Quickly she got to her feet and fled. Unable to stop herself from looking back at the giant whose body fell like water into a fiery wave of death now chasing her. Making it to the hole back out there was no time for the stairs. She pulled her knife free and threw it to the top of the hole. A moment later, in a flash of light she was at the top, the blade in her hand. Turning back Helena blasted the entrance of the tunnel with a flash of light, hoping to slow the giant down. But the fire could not be contained.

Almost at the entrance of the forge she looked back, just in time to see all the debris she dropped on him explode, his flames so powerful to cause the dormant forges to spark to life. Hoping the dwarves had won Helena made for the highway, and the only hope left.

To her relief the battle was basically over. Some of the goblins had tried to break free, but the dwarves simply shot them down with deadly accuracy, having no interest in prisoners. She ran towards the dwarves, but before a word could be spoken the entire highway rocked and bucked with a ground shaking quake. Everyone stopped, goblin and dwarves alike, all turning to face the direction Helena had just came from. Fire spilled from the doorway, followed by one of Morag's giant hands, his fingers burning the stone. Then he revealed himself. His flames spilled forth from the door forming into his giant form.

"Free at last," he delighted, stretching his mighty form for all to see. His voice burned the air. He gazed down at them all, goblins, trolls and dwarves froze in surprise at the giant's appearance. The last of the goblins and trolls fled in terror, pushing past the dwarves who were no longer interested in fighting them. Morag stepped forward, his feet sizzling, and burning the stones beneath him. Only the stone king and his last guard remained to watch. But it was Rhudan who stepped forward, to face down this terrifying foe.

Rhudan followed closely by his personal guard made their way to the giant, while the rest retreated, wanting a good view. How could such a small man hope to fight this giant? Morag watched with interest. To

Helena's surprise Rhudan dismissed his guards who joined the rest of the men.

"You want to challenge me," Morag said in surprise, "I am Morag, lord of flames," he added threateningly. Rhudan did not say anything, but dropped the head of his hammer against the ground causing sparks to hiss off, the hammers power reacted to Morag's taunts. Helena found Alexander, who was watching the spectacle unfold.

"Are you okay?" she asked.

"Yes, I think," he said, struggling to make himself more comfortable, "is that really Morag?" he asked.

"I think so," she answered.

"Nuts," he said, for the first time looking scared. Helena sat beside him, comforted by his presence. With nowhere to go they simply watched, and prayed.

Morag's hand exploded with fire as he conjured a long sword. The swords edge dripping with fire. Rhudan still did not move, but leaned on his giant hammer as though bored. The giant radiated with confidence, but Helena was not so sure, Rhudan did not seem concerned. Then Morag swung his mighty sword, flames flicking through the air with so much speed Helena almost missed it. In a flash of movement

Rhudan raised his hammer high. Their weapons collided with an explosion of fire and light. Rhudan was still standing when the flames cleared, the power of the hammer easily holding the giant at bay. The flames retreated from Rhudan's light, but Morag continued to press harder, and harder. The pressure in the chamber building till it hurt. Morag was about to try something when Rhudan shoved the giant back. Caught by surprise Morag crashed against a building, smashing its stone walls and dropping its many floors. Again, Morag attacked, and again Rhudan easily blocked the sword. He then brandished the hammer at the giant, causing the head to glow bright as the sun, its golden light forcing Morag further back. For the first time the giant looked scared.

"Your still weak from your incarceration son of Surtur!" Rhudan said, "your name will be added to the names of my defeated foes, and Alfgard will rise from your ashes," he added.

Morag began to gather his power, burning brighter and brighter, consuming the air around him with furious rage. Helena had to turn away. Suddenly with a crash, the light flashed out and the highway went dark. Straining to see, more than a blurry vision of the giant now on his knees. The once incendiary flames were gone, leaving only a man with blackened ash for skin. He was breathing heavily, each laboured breath sounded like the gust of wind through a tunnel.

"You're finished giant," Rhudan said. Too weak to move, or even utter a retort Morag just looked at him, and waited for Rhudan to finish him. A chill crept into the air, as darkness descended all around them till, they could see nothing. A moment later the darkness disappeared, and Morag was gone.

Helena was shocked from her stupor with the bellowing fury of Rhudan, his hammer striking the ground so hard the stone shattered. The other dwarves backed away, waiting for his rage to fade. Baldur emerged from the shadows, limping, looking battered and beaten but alive and smiling from ear to ear.

"Are you two okay?" he asked them.

"Good enough," Alexander groaned.

"Glad it's over," Baldur said helping them to their feet. They slowly made their way to the dwarves who gathered round their leader, his rage fading with the cheering sounds of his men.

"Uncle!" Baldur shouted. Rhudan turned to face them. His tired expression replaced with a wide smile, using the hammer to rest on. The two dwarves embraced as Helena and Alexander watched, the tension easing between them as they too held each other.

"Who are the humans?" Rhudan asked Baldur.

"These are knights of the king's order who rescued me," Baldur answered. Rhudan approached them both. While much shorter than them, Helena could not help feeling in awe of him.

"I am lady Helena Romanov, and this is lord Alexander Luga," she introduced.

"Only the kings order would be so bold," Rhudan laughed, "I am the lord of Nidavolir, and now king of Alfgard," he said casually leaning on his hammer, the once bright power now faded back into the cold metal. "I would thank you both for saving my nephew and helping my people," he reached into his pocket and retrieved two small gems, of pure star crystal, "you and the kings order are forever welcome here, and you both are now blood brother and sister," he said with a warm smile. She had no idea what the gems were, but they felt warm and comforting. They both bowed in thanks. Helena finally feeling as though she was going to see home again.

They both sat by the main gate resting, her legs unwilling to move while taking stock of the extraordinary situation. A dwarf healer looked Alexander over, healing the damage left by the magical bonds and burns on his back. The other dwarves, keen to get started were clearing away the remains of battle, and tending to their injured. Rhudan had sent for more soldiers and builders to make the city liveable. Helena could not help wonder what the mortals living above would think if they knew the dwarves were moving in.

Baldur reappeared, now wearing a clean set of clothes. Taking a seat next to them both.

"Wanted to thank you both again, if you had not come...." he tried to say but his voice broke. Helena hugged him, feeling his prickly beard.

"We will see you again Baldur, no doubt Avalon will want to meet your uncle," Alexander said shaking his hand. With the reformation of Alfgard many will want answers, and when the assembly finds out.

"I look forward to it," Baldur said. They said their final farewells, Helena found herself wanting to stay. But the feeling of relief as they passed over the gate's threshold was overwhelming, the idea of seeing the sky again was almost enough to make her run.

Together they emerged back into the museum, leaving the labyrinth of tunnels behind. The magic was still in place concealing the damage in the basement. Deciding they had done enough for the day the order could finish up at the museum, they exited the basement. The manageress was still asleep, none the wiser to what had happened, or how close to destruction they had been. Hard to believe that beneath their feet was a hidden city of dwarves.

"Ready?" Alexander asked.

"Yes," she replied. All Helena wanted now was food, and her bed.

They returned to the point where they arrived, among the long grass and fresh Icelandic air. Alexander recited the spell, activated the portal that had brought them, and in a flash of light they were gone.

Printed in Great Britain
by Amazon